NEW PLAINS REVIEW

I0589701

FALL 2019

New Plains Student Publishing
University of Central Oklahoma
Edmond, Oklahoma

Faculty & Staff

EXECUTIVE EDITOR
Shay Rahm

ASSISTANT EXECUTIVE EDITOR
Jacob Jardell

ASSISTANT TO EXECUTIVE EDITORS
AsJa Cole

PRODUCTION CHIEF
Lani Riana Jones

Editorial Board

EDITOR-IN-CHIEF
Zoe Wright

MANAGING EDITOR
Paul Rainwater

MANAGING DIGITAL EDITORS
Karson Cribley
Augusta Davis

ASSISTANT EDITORS
Robert Abel
Kristen Allen
Logan Cohen
Katelyn Dinh
Alexandra Haubrich
Zane Hearrell
Jacob Jardel
Kaitlin Keesey
Qing Lei
Victoria Mavros
Elizabeth Noel
Mackenzie Prier
Hayley Pryor
Kalie Riley
Devon Smith
Ronna Whitehead

Cover Artists

FRONT
Daniel A Ciochina

BACK
Guilherme Bergamini

NEW PLAINS REVIEW

is edited by students and faculty of the English Department in the College of Liberal Arts at The University of Central Oklahoma. Political, social or artistic commentary represents the views of the writers and artists, and inclusion in the journal does not indicate editorial endorsement or non-endorsement. New Plains Review does not claim to represent the views of the University or its officials.

The image found on the previous page is from a painting titled Phantom Warriors by acclaimed Native American artist and UCO alumnus Sherman Chaddlesone.
© 2019 New Plains Student Publishing Group

Visit our website at newplainsreview.com
Email inquiries to newplainsreview@gmail.com

English Department, Box 184
University of Central Oklahoma
100 North University Drive
Edmond, Oklahoma 73034

Published in USA; printing & manufacturing information can be found on the final page.

ISBN-13: 978-0-9984061-6-9

TABLE OF CONTENTS

TABLE OF CONTENTS

Foreword

It is with much excitement that we welcome you to the Fall 2019 editior of the New Plains Review. Since its inaugural issue in 1986, New Plains has grown to represent the creative works of local and international authors and artists alike. Over the years, our publishing group has also expanded, becoming New Plains Student Publishing in December of 2016. Of course, we wouldn't be able to do any of this without our wonderful contributors, such as photographer Daniel A. Ciochina, who submitted our cover image, "Intoxicant."

As we took on the difficult process of narrowing down our many fantastic submissions, this particular edition gradually became one about change and reflection. For many of our editors, this hit close to home and we can only hope that this edition of New Plains will have the same affect on our readers.

In addition to the works in this journal, we also have a collection of online exclusives— such as videos, audio recordings, and full color art submissions—which can be found at newplainsreview.com.

On behalf of the English Department, College of Liberal Arts, University of Central Oklahoma, we are proud to present the Fall 2019 edition of New Plains Review.

Zoe Wright

Editor in Chief

PONDER BY DANIEL A CIOCHINA
SERIES– DEPTH
(B&W film photography 1800x1200, 2019)

SOAK BY DANIEL A CIOCHINA
SERIES- DEPTH
(B&W film photography 1800x1200, 2017)

INTOXICANT BY DANIEL A CIOCHINA
SERIES- DEPTH
(B&W film photo 1800x1200, 2017)

NO AIR

by Robin Jeffrey

As the mugger's fist connected with the side of his head, Daniel couldn't help but reflect that this was not the worst part of his day.

He fell onto his side in the rain-soaked alleyway. A boot connected with his ribs and he curled in on himself like a burning piece of paper. Water peppered his face and stung at his eyes, which he screwed shut as tight as he could. The mugger landed another kick on his abdomen and Daniel wheezed as all the air left his lungs.

It was the second time today he had been left breathless. This time hurt less.

The mugger knelt on the ground beside him and began patting down his pockets. Daniel did his utmost to stay still, terrified that any movement would be interpreted as a sign of resistance and he would be treated to further violence. He focused on the rain, the feel of it as it hit skin, the smell of it as it mixed with the dirt-caked asphalt around him.

It hadn't been raining a few hours ago. They had been outside on their patio, watching the sun set behind building clouds when Alissa had stood up from the glass table and stated, "I want a divorce."

Daniel swiveled in his chair and stared at his wife.

"Excuse me?"

"I want a divorce," she repeated, blue eyes drilling into his chest. "I've already spoken to a lawyer. I'm sorry." Her gaze flitted to his face and then away again. "I just… I just don't love you anymore, Dan."

Like a carousel struggling to get up to speed, the world around him started to spin. Daniel clutched the glass table with one hand, his mouth falling open. But he had forgotten how to breathe, let alone speak; 43 years of being alive and in an instant, the simple pattern of inhale and exhale was lost to him. His whole life had stuttered and fallen out of sync. He gaped at Alissa, frozen to the spot.

Crossing her arms over her chest, her head falling low between her shoulders, she turned and headed inside. "I'll go and pack. Good-bye, Dan."

Within the hour she was gone, swept away by thunder and a yellow taxi cab. Daniel—his world in ruins—did the only thing he could think of to do. He went for a walk. He didn't care where he went, just so long as one foot landed in front of the other and carried him forward. Which was how he ended up in what was decidedly the wrong part of town on the wrong end of a desperate man's need for a fix.

Back in the present, the mugger gave a triumphant grunt. He had found and freed Daniel's wallet from his back pocket. Daniel didn't have to open his eyes to see the wallet clearly. It was light brown leather, with gold initials stamped into the stretchy skin, thin and discreet; the gift Alissa had gotten for him on their last wedding anniversary, the receptacle which now held the ring she had left behind.

The relief Daniel felt when the man ran away with the wallet in hand was immeasurable. For the first time in hours, air began to return to his lungs.

A MURDER IN SUBURBIA

by Micah L. Thorp

The crows grow in number by the day. Gradually they have displaced the seagulls, pigeons, and other birds that used to dominate the neighborhood. Their grating cries and swirling black masses now rule the rooftops and open spaces between houses on our block. How the crows managed to excise the other birds isn't clear. Crows aren't particularly aggressive or domineering, if anything, they seem largely indifferent to their surroundings, more interested in the internal dynamics of their flock than those around them. They travel in groups, a loud, feckless bunch screeching and cawing at random. Perhaps the other birds left simply out of annoyance.

In any case, the crows' presence is a mystery. Houses in the neighborhood are mostly new, built within the last decade. Sterile lawns lined with carefully coiffed pines and Japanese maples hardly seem a likely place for an infestation. One house, still under construction, seems to be a favorite roost. Work on the house was halted a couple of years ago. It sits without siding, windows, or doors atop a mound of red clay. Rumor has it the owner ran out of money before the house was finished, though I doubt the crows knew about that. Still, the rooftops in the neighborhood all look alike, so it's uncanny how the crows chose to squat on the only unoccupied residence in the neighborhood.

When we moved in, we weren't concerned about crows. My wife wanted a house with a kitchen island and a master on the main floor. I wanted a big garage and a small yard. We landed on a three-story hillcrest modern, with a neighborhood of smaller moderns below and a handful of bigger moderns above.

Everything in the neighborhood is manicured and clean, including the neighbors. No houseless souls wander among curbside trash bins on pickup day. The Homeowner's Association leaves written warnings on the door of any property whose lawn is left shaggy and weed filled, or if a recycling bin is visible from the street.

Yet even the Homeowner's Association can't seem to expel the crows.

The discord sown among neighbors about what to do about the crows is palpable. No one has an answer, but everyone has ideas. Some neighbors have adorned their rooftops with realistic plastic owls. Others placed blinking lights at the corners of their yards. One house even put a scarecrow near their front door, looking like a forgotten Halloween decoration. The crows remain unmoved. The plastic owls are slowly pecked to bits. The blinking lights are as much an attraction as deterrent. Last week I saw a crow sitting atop the scarecrow's head.

The mob mentality of the birds doesn't do much to dispel neighborhood concerns. As a group, the birds are a completely uninhibited crowd, an affront to carefully drawn lots, boutiques, and strip malls. Crows are indifferent to relationships, they pillage as a group and show no separation of identity. They seem quite at home in suburbia.

Both my wife and I grew up in the sticks, and then migrated to the city as young adults. Ours is a second marriage, a restart of relationships. With three kids between us, we longed for a place of organized stability, without the grit of urban or rural life, where life was soft. We looked for a place to merge as a family, to meld as one. We thought we had found it in suburbia.

But blending families is hard. Kids squabble and manipulate. The wife and I are in a constant cycle of emotional and verbal antagonism, followed by reconciliation. The walls of our house shield the turmoil from the street and the distance between houses is enough to muffle even the loudest fights.

Shortly after we moved in, I saw a photograph of the bog and forest that had been replaced by our neighborhood. It looked like the cover of a hiking guidebook with a small stream, scattered pines, and Douglas-firs covered with moss. To maintain some semblance of the façade in the photograph, the developers left a few "wetland" areas carefully fenced off and untouched. A chain link fence with a narrow gravel path around each one ensures a boundary between the unkempt wild and the rest of the neighborhood. The fenced wild is untouched by the crows.

I'm not sure what attracted the crows to this place. Whatever the reason, they fly through the torn social fabric of the neighborhood, cawing at the perfect homes, swirling above the caged turmoil below.

I'LL SEE YOU IN MY DREAMS

by Shilo Niziolek

I'm almost thirty years old and hardly anyone I've loved has died. My grandmother died of a heart attack when I was a child. Two friends from high school, who were cousins, died in two separate winters from heroin overdoses. And Jeremy, one of my first friends from elementary school, and my first real boyfriend, died from cancer that he defeated numerous times, until it appeared in his lungs and took his life at twenty-seven. He is the only one who haunts me in my sleep. Each day I see the picture of him as an adult on a magnet on my fridge. That is how I dream of him, as a man I never knew.

*****

At twenty-seven years old, I did something new. I stood in the shower, faucet turned off, cupped my hands together, the shape of a beating heart. Soaking wet, hair dripping, I opened a little hole in the center of my fists and let the last drops fall off the leaky faucet into the cavern. When I opened my hand, there was no hidden pool of lukewarm water. It had all seeped through.
This is what my grief is like. I am a closed fist. I do the laundry. The laundry never ends. Wash, dry, fold, repeat. The daythat I got the message, Wednesday September 20th, I had been waiting with that quiet trepidation one feels when they are waiting for news they knew would come, but never wanted to hear. I did not cry. An old friend, the same friend who had told me that Jeremy had been put into hospice care a week and a half prior, sent the message. Well, that's it Shilo… After I read it, something came to me that I had forgotten, a dream I had the night before.

*****

I walked through the streets of Cody, Wyoming. They were the same: the two hills surrounded by flat lands, the old mansion at the bottom of one of the hills that everyone used to say gave out jumbo size Halloween treats, but the year we finally went there we got one dinky candy each, the football field and tennis courts to the right of the high school, the city park in the middle of town, the skatepark that my friends had raised all the funds for and helped design with the help of the Tony Hawk Skatepark committee. That's where he was. Jeremy was in his hospice bed, but he didn't look like the ghost of the boy I used to know as he did recently on a photo on Facebook. His face wasn't sunken in by the chemo and trial stem-cell replacement treatment he had weathered. He was the same boy I moved away from at fifteen when my family came to Oregon. His hair was long down past his shoulders and had the signature curl in the front that always made me think of the Amish. It was dyed hot pink, like the highlights I had at fourteen when we were dating. Jeremy the first boy who ever kissed me. Just a peck kiss. Only four times in the two years before I moved away.

In the dream, I crawled into the hospital bed with him and nuzzled up to his side. We laughed about his hair, he said he did it just like mine. I can't remember all the things we talked about. The dream stretched on forever, the sun shone down on the bed and his face was bright and filled with light. "I'm ready to go. It's okay. I am happy now," he said, and he kissed me for the first time. It was not the silly kisses from our childhood, stolen quickly and randomly, and me lacking in their wake. I felt this kiss through my veins, and we laughed afterwards like we had a great secret to keep. And then I got up and walked away, and when I turned to look at him,

6

he was smiling a giant grin, and then he was gone.

*****

I sat up in my bed at 5:00AM. Today is the day, I thought. And it was.

Afterwards, I did not cry. In fact, I still haven't cried. I've gotten the water welling in the pit of my eye, but I haven't let it fall. Grief is a million-letter word. Since that moment, I have learned that he passed away on Tuesday, September 19th... I do not subscribe to any specific religion. I believe there is something out there, but I can't pretend to know what. When I told my Mom what happened she told me that he came to prepare me. How he knew, after all these years with no contact, no visits, no letter or calls, that I would need preparing for his death, I do not know. I believe that he knew I loved him, that I have always loved him. He was my first love. I often wonder what would have happened if I had never moved to Oregon, never become whatever this is that I am. Would we have stayed together? Would he have been my first in many more things than small delicate kisses? Would we have gone to college together, gotten married? But some things wouldn't matter, some things wouldn't have changed. He would have fought his first battle with testicular cancer at seventeen and won. He would have fought it again, and then again, only to find out that although they thought they had removed all the cancer, it still seeped into his lungs. And I would have still gotten sick as well. What a pair we would have made.

I can't pretend to know anything. I feel I do not have a license to my grief.

When I moved from Wyoming, I essentially evicted everyone I loved from my life, slowly, and then all at once. I called less and less, letters tapered off, emails halted. I broke up with Jeremy three weeks after arriving in Astoria, Oregon over the phone. We were fifteen. There was no way to sustain a long-term relationship, and frankly I was consumed by my losses, and by my hope. I had yet to make any new friends in Astoria, but I had dreams of the new people I would meet, of falling in love in this forest filled world with the ocean as our background. Jeremy said he understood, he knew it was only a matter of time too. The night before I moved away with my family, I had a going away party at my friend Brandon's house, the same friend who sent me the message when Jeremy passed away. It was the one time in my whole childhood that I could have a sleepover with all my guy friends, because that's what we were, what we had always been. Me and fifteen boys. Those boys were my family. They were my brothers. Jeremy wasn't allowed to stay the night. His mother wasn't fond of me. Mothers know, they can see a hurricane before it has finished brewing. She must have known that I would eventually destroy the things around me, and for this, I am grateful that I moved away. You can't destroy something that no longer exists. That whole night of the party I cried off and on, and for a girl who never cries, that was something. I could feel it in the air, everything was ending. I was in a state of becoming. We all were. Fifteen years old is an age where everything is changing already, and when I left, I took a part of each of them with me.

I am still waiting for the date of the memorial. I looked up round trip tickets to Denver, where I already have four offers of lodging from three of the boys that I haven't had contact with for years.One was even from my best friend Derek, who is the only friend who refused to let me let him go. Two hundred seventeen dollars. That's how cheap a ticket is. I could have been there. I could have been seeing all these old friends at least once a year. I could have visited

Jeremy when I knew things were getting bad. I could have been there before, instead of after. I had never even bothered to check the price of tickets. I always thought there would be more time. Isn't that our main human error? How did I think this? Me, who has my own experiences with illness, whose own heart has stopped twice before? Why do people call them the five steps of grief? For me they seem all combined. I will be twenty-eight in December. Every year my birthday is a gift. This year it will be eight years since I died on the operating table and they brought me back to life. I can't pretend that I am always a good person. I have done things for which I can never be forgiven. I have broken people on purpose. I have desired others to feel my pain. Somewhere out there is a battlefield with all my lived and unlived sins. My mind thinks things it never should.It betrays even my best intentions. I have locked doors filled with treason, with demons, with things I have left unsaid. Jeremy was light. He was the best of us. He was kind. He had a passion for extreme sports, but that desire to seek adventurous thrills never crossed over into the dark borders where so many live: addicts, junkies, cruel and dangerous people. I will tuck this away deep inside my crevices. I will cry in my sleep. I will deal with this by not dealing with this. I will kiss the boy I never knew as a man in my dreams.

*****

The flight was delayed until 7:00AM the next morning, which would put me into Denver, Colorado at 10:20AM, just enough time for my friend Derek to pick me up and drive to Laramie, Wyoming where the celebration of life was to take place. I was determined to be there for Jeremy as I hadn't been in life.The next day I flew out just as the sunshine was waking up. The clouds were giant fluffy mountains and the pinks and yellows of the sunrise horizon that we flew into reached out across the lands. On the day of the memorial it was a gift, seeing the world from the realm I like to imagine on lazy summer days.

Seeing Derek was enough to ease a bit of the sharp pain I felt pressing into my chest for the last month. Being with him let out a bit of acrid air. As we got in the car and looked at the blue skies and the Rocky Mountains I said, "It doesn't feel like a day for memorials." Everything was too blue. Not a melancholy blue, but a bright blue, a shooting star blue, a bite of vanilla cake with buttercream frosting blue, the blue of a boy who joked around and loved to laugh from birth until death.

The memorial wasn't a memorial. It was a wake. It was at a bar, apparently it was Jeremy's bar, attached to a liquor store in the surreal way Wyoming has about it. Everyone slowly drank themselves into oblivion except me. There were more faces in there that I didn't know than ones I did. I couldn't help being a bit disappointed in the ghosts of my friends. Why weren't they there? Where was their loyalty? But then again, where was mine? A few of the boys who I had thought of as brothers were there. They were taller than I remembered, though they had surely always been a great deal taller than me, but now they had the broad shoulders of men, the filled out faces with beards that at fifteen they couldn't grow. After a good three minutes, the awkwardness dissipated.We slipped back into our roles as a family. Roles forged in lines outside the classrooms, and during chases around the monkey bars and through the soccer fields, and over the sounds of rows and rows of lockers slamming, and through snappy jokes at each other's expense. It almost felt the same except it didn't.There were only six to our previous numbers of around twenty. Some of the boys were married, others in long standing committed relationships. One had just finished his doctorate, another one announcing he had a baby on the way, but

Jeremy's face was plastered in picture frames, photo albums, and a slideshow. Goofy moments echoing throughout the room. A mom, sister, and father with water sometimes leaking from their eyes. A twin brother often hushing everyone by yelling, "We have to seize the day, like Jeremy. He'd want us to seize the day,"all while kicking chairs over, flipping a table, and at one point saying, "Grief is like a monster. It comes for you when you wake up in the morning, it bares its teeth throughout the middle of the day."Later he came and stood next to me and I leaned my face against the spikes on his signature black jacket. The pressure felt good on my cheek and for a moment I was hugging both twins at once, there inside the one whose body was left behind, but whose pain was scratching at his insides, seeping out through his pores. I couldn't help noticing how handsome he had become, how broken and beautiful he seemed in this adult body. He felt like a character right out of one of my favorite books. A boy who had grown to be a man who killed many people in war and lost the other half of himself to the beast of cancer, and who was so blasted lovely in his despair, that a woman would perform a number of sins just to ease his heart for a few blissful moments.And when he'd disappear before the morning had arisen, the women would never be surprised or regretful but would probably fall in love with his absence or the way he cried in his sleep. He whispered in my ear, "there has to be life after death." I looked him in the eye and told him that I thought there was even more life after death, that in death our life is no longer constrained by our bodies, we can move through all the realms with ease.His eyes crinkled at the edges,with lines I hadn't noticed before. He gave me one last hug, and then walked over and started a wrestling match with one of his friends, right there on the bar floor. I understand the need to confront, even momentarily, and then push away our own grief.

Grief is a monster, he had said.

At some point in the night, Jeremy's mom came over to me. A woman who I was aware didn't like me as a fifteen-year-old girl who was dating her son. I often wore short-shorts and tight, low cut tank tops that showed off the new, large breasts I had recently inherited from my family tree. I was sure she wouldn't even recognize me and had made a joke to Derek on the drive down there how I was incognito with my red hair instead of the light blonde hair of my childhood. She came over and gave me a hug, "Shilo, where did you come down from?" I told her I had flown into Denver from Portland, Oregon, where Derek picked me up, and a smile almost touched her eyes. She said, "I can't believe you flew all the way here, but I found a scrapbook you made for Jeremy when you were younger this last week, and I knew that you would want to see it."

"Of course,"I said."How could I not be here?"She squeezed my hand and gripped her drink tightly, her fingers turning bone white, and we shared a moment of recognition, a flash of Jeremy as he had been when he was young, a silhouette passed between us. Later, I would use a friend's car to give his mom, dad, and aunt a ride to their motel. The whole entire trip was worth that moment to me, to give them something, no matter how small or unremembered, to give something back to Jeremy's family, for all the parts of us he took with him when he passed. "Drive safe back to Cody," I said.

Two days later, when I flew home in the middle of the night, there was a rainstorm in Oregon. The flashing red light on the edge of the wing illuminated, in brief moments, what rain looks like in the center of a cloud, like a thousand moments encapsulated into one form, into one body, a flash of tiny daggers struck frozen in the dark night sky. I pressed my face against the window and imagined what would happen if the window popped out and all the air was sucked from the plane and hundreds of strangers who were flying to or from something, or who were simply coming home. I could feel the clouds surrounding us.I was in the very last row, the far window seat.The turbulence from the storm shook me up like a pop can.

The rain and clouds faded out, "We are making our descent," the captain said. The Columbia River looked up at me, inky black, snaking its way across the ground. Hello, beautiful monster.

*****

MAD LIGHT

by Rex Adams

The footsteps in the hallway are too heavy to be Lila's. They stop outside the door. The knob clicks. The door opens. Loud music, drunken voices, and her mother's shrill laughter chase the light through the room. In the doorway stands Neil. She can smell him, his nauseating cologne that doesn't quite mask the stale, onion stench of his flesh. She clamps her eyes tight and holds her breath, hoping that if she stays still long enough he won't be able to take anything from her, no more than he already has. Softly the door closes and footfalls approach. She can't stay still.

*****

Lila touches her hair. "He won't hurt us anymore," she whispers, her face surrounded by a curly reddish-blonde mop. Her blue eyes are two moons shining with an intense light amidst a galaxy of freckles. "Come on." She tugs at Jen's hand.

Lila leads Jen out of the cluttered bedroom, down the hall, into the blazing lights of the living room. Jen watches for Neil, expecting him to appear, but he doesn't. Their mother is the only adult they see. She is face down on a beanbag chair, her auburn hair still holding the memory of hot rollers, a cigarette butt on the floor near her outstretched hand, with a black dot burned into the carpet around the scorched filter. She stops, says quietly, "Mom?"

"She ain't waking up, Jen." Lila tugs at her hand, leading her into the kitchen. Beer cans and vodka bottles litter the countertops and the surface of a wobbly-legged table. They continue on into the mudroom. "Dad's coming for us," Lila says. "He'll be here soon." Lila drags her along, out of the house onto the porch and across the yard.

*****

They huddle together in the bar ditch. A cold breeze riffles through the sagebrush lit silver by starlight. Jen wears a nightgown and sandals with no jacket or socks. She shivers in Lila's arms. "Dad's coming," Lila says.

The drone of a diesel engine reaches them before the van's red marker lights breach the horizon. The girls step to the edge of the blacktop. The drone grows to a growl. Headlights break over them, a blinding light that blinks out the markers and the rest of the night. They step closer to the fog line, expecting the rattle of the Jake brake. But it doesn't happen. The truck blares its horn and the lights jerk to the left. The girls stumble back onto the shoulder and the semi blows past. A frigid wake washes over them.

"I thought it was him," Lila says.

At the house, the door swings open, dropping a rectangle of light across the yard. Their mother stands in the doorway, her shadow a cutout in the light painted on the lawn. "Lila! Jen!" she hollers. Her loud, harsh voice destroying the night. "Where you at?"

Jen turns, ready to holler back, when Lila squeezes her. "Don't."

Another truck approaches, this one bobtailing. Their mother is on the porch now and then off stumbling their way. Neil's shadow appears in the doorway. The truck slows. Neil steps off the porch, following their mother.

The semi stops a few feet down the road. Jen and Lila move as one into the beam of light. The air brakes hiss, little swirls of dust pluming around the wheels. Their father steps out of the truck and walks into the light. His shadow falls over them. He squats down, pushes his stockman cowboy hat back and rolls his toothpick into the corner of his mouth. Lila lets go of Jen and throws her arms around his neck, nearly bumping the stockman off his head. "Well, I missed you, too," he says. Then he reaches a big hand out and grabs Jen's arm pulling her toward him. He engulfs her in his embrace. Spearmint on his breath. He's not like Neil, not slathered with cologne to hide the hideousness that lurks under his skin. Instead, her father's scent fills her up with so much warmth it hurts and makes her cry. He picks them both up. He kisses their foreheads. They cling to him while he opens the door. He sets them on the running board, tells them to step in.

Lila says, "Don't leave us in here alone, Dad." Lila sounding desperate, vulnerable, sounding like Jen has never heard her sound before.

Jen looks over his shoulder. Their mother staggers across the yard. "You son of a bitch, you can't take them girls." Behind her Neil stalks on socked feet, his white shirt untucked, his black greased-back hair coming unraveled, strands of it over his white forehead.

As their father eases out of Jen and Lila's embrace he says, "Get in and warm up." "Dad?" Lila says.

"Go ahead."

The cab feels almost hot against Jen's cold skin. They crawl through the curtain into the sleeper, pull blankets over them that carry the clean, comforting scent of their father.

The drone of the idling diesel engine is not loud enough to blot out the sound of their mother yelling hysterically and cursing out their father, who doesn't respond, has never responded. Jen crawls out of the sleeper.

"You son of a bitch," Neil says, "Get them girls out of that truck. Them girls ain't yours no mo—." His voice stops abruptly. Jen peers out the window. Her father has Neil in a headlock, his fist pounding into Neil's face, her father's elbow driving the fist like a piston. Their mother hits their father on the back and head, still yelling hysterically. His hat topples off. He lets Neil go, steps back and pushes their mother away. She falls, gets back up.

"Look at you," he says. "What happened to you?"

Their mother is at him again. He pushes her down, stoops and picks his hat up and walks around the truck and gets in. He settles into his seat and runs the palm of his hand over his head and puts his hat on. His breaths are ragged and heavy. He smiles weakly at Jen. "Get in the back with your sister." His toothpick is missing.

"But I want to sit up here by you."

He takes a deep breath, says, "All right, sis. I need a good copilot anyway."

Then they are traveling and he's running through the gears and Jen thinks, I should have told him what Neil did. He really would have hurt him then. He would have killed Neil. I should have told him.

Soon, Lila crawls out of the sleeper and sits next to her sister in the bucket seat. The three of them watch the night roll by.

*****

She stands next to Lila in their father's house with the warm carpeted floor on her bare feet. He stands in front of them holding a wet washcloth.

"You girl's look like you haven't had a bath in a week."

Probably two, is what Jen wants to say. He leans down and gently wipes their faces with the cloth. He spends a lot of time under their noses rubbing away the crusted snot.

*****

Steaming water runs into the tub. Shirtsleeves rolled up, he holds his hand under the faucet. Overhead a light bulb hums. The room radiates white with its light, hurting Jen's eyes.

"That's pretty good. Try it out."

He pulls his dripping hand away. Lila immediately pokes her hand into the water. She jerks it away just as quickly. "Too hot."

"Jen, what do you think?"

She reaches in tentatively.

"Hot," she says.

"You girls don't like a hot bath? No problem." The knobs squeal when he adjusts them. He sticks his big knuckled hand back in, pulls it out. Small cuts mar the knuckles. "How about now?"

Lila jabs her hand in. "Just right," she says.

"Jen?" he says, nodding her toward the water.

She leans in carefully, nudges her hand in, lets the warmth crawl up her arm. She pulls it out, nods her head.

"Ok." He plugs the drain, stands up and looks down at them. He has a new toothpick in the corner of his mouth. "Lila, can you turn the water off when it's full?" Lila nods. "Good. There's shampoo and soap." He touches both of their heads, kneels down in front of them and pulls them against him. "I got you girls now." Then he lets loose and stands. "Almost forgot towels." He walks to the sink and opens the cupboard under it. He pulls out two white towels. Clean and crisp. Jen can already smell the laundry soap in them. He sets them on top of the toilet lid, which is right next to the tub. The room fills with steam, the vapor shimmering on the mirror over the sink. The sound of the running water echoing in the small, humid space.

"I'll be out in the kitchen. I don't have much for pajamas, but I'll think of something."

*****

In the tub she faces Lila. Lila holds her hands. Steam rises up between them. Lila's hair still holds its relentless curl although it is sopping wet and stuck to her skull. Her blue eyes burn within the galaxy of freckles that cover her face.

"We are good now. No more Neil," Lila says.

"I'm not sure," says Jen. "What if they come for us?"

"Nobody is coming for us." Lila's light grows and simmers and burns so hot that it frightens Jen. "Nobody can hurt us now." Jen starts crying. Lila squeezes her puckered hands. "Stop that, Jen. Stop crying. Crying doesn't do us any good."

"Maybe Neil is dead."

"I hope so."

"Maybe Dad killed him."

"I hope so."

*****

Dressed in their father's white undershirts, they stand in the doorway of the kitchen. Their father stands at the stove stirring a pot full of boiling franks and beans. The shirts fit like gowns. Jen's coming down just below her knees and Lila's just above. They both wear a pair of his tube socks, which are pulled up past the bottom of the shirts. The makeshift nightgowns smell fresh and laundered.

Without turning he says, "You girls better get in here and eat."

They step into the kitchen and walk to the table, tugging at the socks to keep them from slipping down.

Their father ladles beans and franks from the pot into two bowls. He sets them in front of the girls. Jen feels the heat from the bowl on her face. Next he takes two clean glasses from a cupboard and sets them on the counter. He opens the fridge and pulls out a carton of milk and fills the glasses. He sets them down in front of the girls. The hand clutching Jen's glass is the one nicked from beating Neil's face. Jen prays he is dead, but then if her father did kill him, what would they do with her father? Surely they would take him away and lock him up in prison. The thought of living her whole life without her father makes her even more scared than the thought of Neil.

*****

Bowls empty. Milk half drunk. Their father sits at the table, not eating. Instead, he drinks coffee, watching his daughters with a slight grin on his lips and in his eyes. He hooks a knobby finger through the handle of the coffee cup, lifts it to his lips and sips. His hat hangs from the one vacant chair at the table. His hair is thin and wispy, but combed back neatly. "Wasn't much of a meal. I'll get some chicken tomorrow and fry it up. How's that sound?"

Both girls nod their heads. Lila says, "Real good, Dad."

Somebody knocks at the door. Jen looks up at it, a wooden, glass-paned door. Standing outside under the porch light is Sheriff Ferguson. Jen looks back to her father. The grin is still on his lips but has left his eyes. The sheriff knocks again. Her father doesn't say anything. Doesn't move. Acts like he doesn't hear the knocking.

"Better drink that milk. It'll get warm. Nobody likes warm milk."

Another knock followed by Sheriff Ferguson's voice, "Lloyd, open the door. I can see you and those girls sitting there."

"Drink up, girls."

"Lloyd," calls the man again.

This time their father glances from the table to the door, but still he doesn't move.

The man knocks harder, the door rattling. "All right, I'm coming in." Sheriff Ferguson, a tall, skinny man wearing a cowboy hat over black-rimmed glasses, turns the knob and throws his wiry body into the door. The door was never locked, so it swings in and Ferguson nearly falls through it. He catches himself, stands up straight and nods at the girls, adjusting the gun at his belt and then says to their father, "You know why I'm here."

"We'll talk about it in a minute. Let them finish their milk."

The sheriff looks back at the girls. "They are a couple of beauties. They sure's heck don't look anything like you."

"Coffee?"

"Sure."

Their father points to a cupboard above the coffeemaker. "Cups are in there."

"Awful late for dinner, isn't it girls?" the sheriff says to them.

Lila flashes her burning eyes at him. They are always burning. Jen wishes the same fire burned in her.

"They're about done."

The sheriff gets a cup down and fills it. When he's standing next to the table again he says, "Girls, I need to talk to your daddy for a minute. Grown-up talk. You gals mind going in the other room?"

"We're used to grown-up talk," Lila says.

"Finish up your milk and get to bed. I'll be there in a minute," says their father.

*****

Standing next to the bedroom door, listening, they can hear the two men at the table. Sheriff Ferguson speaks first.

"You know they can't stay here."

"They are."

"They can't."

"They can't go back to her and that Neil character."

"The court ordered it. You know that."

"Nadine's not who she used to be. She's not the same woman. That's what you know."

"That ain't my matter. My matter is I need

to get those girls and take them back to their mother."

"Well, you can go ahead and try. They're right there in that bedroom. Go ahead and try and get them. We'll see how far you get."

"There's the other matter, too. What you did to her husband."

"Is he dead?"

"No."

"I'm sorry."

"No, you're not. Then you'd never get to see those girls." There's the sound of a coffee cup set on the table. "You worked him over pretty good. I've got to take you in for that."

"Those are my girls in there. They shouldn't be with her, or him."

"Maybe so, but you know it don't work that way."

Jen whispers, "Are they taking us back?" Lila shushes her.

"Well, you can come for them, but you better not come alone."

A chair scrapes across the floor. A dish rattles in the sink. "Lloyd, I'm sorry, I really am. But it's the way it's got to be. I'm trying to do this quiet, without a bunch of state folks coming in here." Sheriff Ferguson pauses before he speaks again. "Listen, you could get it two ways. You could get it for kidnapping, too."

"Kidnapping? My own girls?"

"Yeah. I think I talked Nadine out of that one. But that Neil? He isn't going to let the beating you gave him go. So just make it easy. Maybe this goes away. Maybe you can work a joint deal with Nadine or something. The state's starting to do that sort of thing." The sheriff stops speaking. There's another pause. Then their father speaks.

"Don't come back alone, that's all I got to say."

*****

22

The two girls lie in their father's bed, in sheets that hold no mustiness, no stink of cigarettes, no reek of Neil. Jen hasn't slept as hard and sound as she just did since before the first time Neil's footfalls stopped in front of her door.

Their father woke them and now he stands in front of the open closet, big hands on his hips. He looks over his shoulder at the girls, shifts the toothpick to the other corner of his mouth.

"You girls want to go somewhere?" he asks.

"No," Lila says immediately.

"Where?" asks Jen.

"It'll be a surprise, but it'll be fun. I guarantee that."

"I just want to stay here for a while," Lila says.

"Me, too, but we need to go for a drive. Need to see some new country. Who doesn't like seeing new country?"

He slides a suitcase down from the top shelf. He sets it on the foot of the bed and clicks it open. He goes to a tall oak dresser against a plaster wall and opens a drawer. He takes out white socks, white underwear and white t-shirts from the drawer and places them in the suitcase.

While they slept he washed their dingy clothing. Now the clothes are folded neatly on top of the dresser. Their father nods at them. "They're clean, girls. They'll do until we can go shopping. You girls want to do some shopping? Maybe in Spokane?"

There is a knock on the door. Jen knows it is Sheriff Ferguson.

*****

Their father stands next to the table in the kitchen, legs spread, his black, polished boots placed with the left slightly forward from the right. The two girls stand behind him. The door opens and the sheriff and four deputies stream in. Behind them the sky has begun to gray.

The sheriff stands in the kitchen facing their father. The deputies line up beside him.

"Lloyd," says the sheriff, "make this easy. If you come in easy you got a chance to get them girls. If you don't. Well, who knows what will happen."

"I got them girls now. Why would I give them up?"

The sheriff nods to one of the deputies. "All right. Get those girls. Be gentle. They've already been through a lot."

The deputy, a young man with a mustache and bushy sideburns, steps forward. He looks to Lloyd. Their father says, "Don't touch them girls, Prater." The deputy looks over to the sheriff, uncertainty all over his face. The sheriff nods. The deputy steps forward.

*****

One deputy has a knee driven into the back of their father's neck, pressing his face into the floor. Her father has a hand stretched out, reaching for Jen, fresh nicks on the knuckles, the index finger disjointed and skewed. Another deputy grabs the outstretched arm around the wrist and heaves on it, hauling it around behind her father's back. Both deputies hatless now, hair ruffled, chests heaving, eyes swelling shut, a torn ear weeping blood. Cuffs are snapped around her father's wrists. A third deputy holds Lila off the floor, who is swearing and kicking. The long tube socks have slipped down to her ankles and are streaming through the air like thick, white ribbons. Their father gasps, his breath gurgling through all the blood that comes from his mouth. Blood trickles down into his eye, drips from his long lashes. He attempts to blink it away. Prater is on the floor snoring, not far from Jen, not far from where he stooped to pick her up and then her father's big fist came down on the side of his head.

Sheriff Ferguson kneels in front of her, panting. His glasses are missing and there's a cut over his eye, running at an angle through his thick, gray eyebrows. He dropped the short, black stick he struck their father with. The blow that finally felled him. Now, he reaches out to her. "Come here, honey. I'm sorry. I really am."

*****

Her mother is on the porch dressed in a bathrobe, smoking, her head a globe of rollers wrapped in a hairnet. Jen stands next to the patrol car staring at the door behind her mother, praying Neil is dead, gone. But then the door opens and there he is, his head disfigured, purple and bulbous, but still walking and living. His injuries making him even more monstrous. Jen sobs. Lila grabs her by the shoulders and shakes her.

"Stop it, Jen. He can't hurt us no more. I won't let him."

But Jen can't stop sobbing because she knows that it doesn't matter how bright Lila's mad light burns, it can't protect her from the monster who has just stepped off the porch and is walking toward her.

GRANDPA'S LAST STAND

by STEPHAN LANG

I buried my wife. We didn't have a fancy service for her like you might see on TV for a celebrity, dignitary, or some famous politician. Edie wouldn't have liked that. Yet it was still more hoopla than would have been my preference. Had it been up to me, I would have ditched the service and planted her in the garden under our favorite California pepper tree. Unfortunately, our son Mark bullied his way to the forefront. He insisted that we have a church service and graveside ceremony, mumbling something about God, our backyard, and the law.

Pastor Bob concluded his graveside remarks and Mark announced that lunch would be served inside. There was really no need; most people had already broken into their quickest version of a sprint to the Fellowship Hall. I meandered in the opposite direction towards the wooded knoll overlooking the river to reminisce about Edie and grab a smoke. The river used to be wide with a swift flow until they dammed it up about 20 miles upstream back in '76. Edie and I liked to swim in a little pool on a secluded bend in the river concealed by a stand of Cottonwood trees. Pastor John caught us skinny dipping there one day, much to Edie's chagrin. Being witnessed by the pastor didn't bother her so much, but she was horrified by the prospect of Pastor John disclosing our indiscretion to her parents. Pastor Johnny Reb, so nicknamed by the kids on account of his Southern accent, gave us a good scolding. But he kept our little secret. Pastor John married us a few months later. Edie squeezed my hand and couldn't hold back a smile when Pastor John shot us both a well-timed wink at the altar. That was sixty-eight years ago.

Mark and our daughter-in-law Julie

interrupted my reverie. Julie asked how I was holding up. Before I could reply, Mark chimed in while swatting away the smoke emanating from my cigarette.

"Now that mom is gone, there is really no need to continue that awful habit. You know those things are going to kill you someday." Mark said.

I hesitated to respond. The solemnity of the occasion demanded civility. But propriety is a threadbare costume in the closet of a man my age. "I'm 91 years old, and you advise that I cease smoking now? My dear mother died at age 94. She consumed jelly beans like a humpback whale swallowing an entire school of mackerel in a single gulp. She smoked at least two cigarettes for every fistful of jelly beans, and that was no small number. Are you suggesting that had she dumped the beans and the fags at 91, she might have made it to 95?"

Mark continued swishing and swash-buckling the smoke with the back of his hand. Talk about a drama king. Julie put her arm around me and said, "Let's go inside, dad. Everyone would like to see you." It was a kind gesture, even if I craved nothing other than solitude. Julie was always the amiable, non-confrontational one in the family. Not sure how she ended up with Mark.

The atmosphere in the Fellowship Hall was jovial, dry, and warm. I strolled through the room and talked to several family members and well-wishers. Mark tapped my shoulder from behind, Julie at his side. Mark checked in as the hundredth or so person to ask me, "How are you doing?" or "How are you holding up?" Before I could spew the stock answer, he ripped the shrouds off his true mission.

"It will certainly be lonely with nobody left to talk to," Mark said. "What are you planning to do with yourself now that you no longer have mom to care for?"

Julie cringed at the sight of another confrontation brewing between her father-in-law and her husband. "I'm sure I'll find something to keep myself busy, Mark," I said.

"I suppose you will want to sell that big house and find something smaller. Perhaps an assisted-care facility would suit you well," Mark said.

And so the onslaught continued. Mark had been leading the charge pressuring me to move into a nursing home for years; even though I'd been taking good care of Edie for the past ten years all by myself. Just as I concluded that I may not be able to come up with a second civil response; Julie saved the day. "We'd love it if you would come live closer to us," Julie said. "You could see the great grandkids play soccer and baseball, share family meals and we could visit each other regularly." The sincerity in her voice, and genuineness of her words captivated my interest. Until she added, "And we have a very nice Sunshine Manor just down the road that we think you would like."

I seethed inside, but concealed my anger. Edie wouldn't have appreciated a family fight on the day of her funeral. I'd lived in my house for nearly sixty years without any help from them. I would never move to a nursing home, not for Mark or Julie nor anybody else. The only person that would ever get me out of my house would be the mortician. But Julie was too sweet to intervene, so I did the gentlemanly thing and excused myself to the restroom. I walked straight through the washroom, and out the exterior door. I shuffled through the parking lot and plopped into my car. My phone dinged and I glanced down at a notification of the DMV appointment I'd forgotten to cancel. I turned the phone off and drove home.

* * * * * * *

A few months later there was a harsh knock on the front door, one of those knocks that levitates you off your chair and sends cold chills spiraling throughout your body. The next knock demanded immediate attention. Had I owned a gun, I would have fetched it before answering the door. But Edie stipulated long ago that all guns be removed from the house.

I answered the door empty handed. A young, curly haired man with a cavalier, wise guy smirk on his face pointed to a name on his clipboard and asked if that was me. In retrospect, I should have denied ever knowing that fellow and suggested that he had the wrong house. But without thinking, I merely nodded my head in the affirmative.

He yanked an envelope out of his back pocket and said with all the sincerity of a mass murderer, "Sorry old man, but you're served." Then he whacked the subpoena against my chest and stomped away.

I used to think that the worst thing that could ever happen to a parent was to have one of their children pre-decease them. Wow, I was sure wrong. Death comes to everyone. But very few parents ever experience their kids turning on them. I read the notice of Mark's Application for Guardianship three times before the impact of his treachery set in. The subpoena to schedule the required psychological examination added a final exclamation point to the insult.

I would've thought he'd be more appreciative of all that his mother and I'd done for him over the years. Mark had always resented my long absences during his childhood. He reminded me of that from time to time. But I was a Colonel in the Marines and had no control of where I was deployed. He knew that. I was just doing my sworn duty. But Mark contended that my duty should have been to the family. Perhaps somewhere deep inside, the guardianship application was Mark's way of paying me back.

Pity after all these years.

Even as a child, Mark was always the responsible one. Not only for himself, but for anybody else he deemed to be in need of his counsel. It took a lot of damn gall for him to think he had the right to step in and take over my life. But Mark never suffered from a lack of arrogance. This time, he'd gone too far.

I knew if Mark ever obtained guardianship over my life, the first thing he would do is throw me into one of those nursing homes. I'll never forget visiting my uncle Ralph in one of those hell-holes, the stench of antiseptic death percolating through the halls. He sat in a chair all day, head bent over his knees, with drool hanging from his mouth. That's not the way I planned on spending my final days.

I wandered out to the back yard, settled into my favorite Adirondack chair and lit a cigarette. I didn't start smoking until my 85th birthday. I remember the day well. My wife of 62 years wobbled into the kitchen after dinner, her robe dangled upon her shoulders exposing mismatched pajama tops and bottoms. She seemed somewhat disoriented, like a sleepwalker awoken in the back yard at three in the morning after stumbling over a misplaced chair. I'd grown accustomed to the bewildered look. She asked whose birthday cake was sitting on the table. When I replied that it was my cake, she smiled and wished me "happy birthday." Then she inquired as to what I was doing in her house.

I assured her that it was our house and that we'd been sharing it for over 50 years. She didn't respond. I don't think she really believed me. Edie had been getting more and more forgetful. But at that moment, I felt her slipping away from me. I offered to brew her a cup of tea, but she said she was tired and wanted to go to bed. She rambled out of the kitchen, then turned back and stared at me for the longest moment. She said I looked familiar, but she couldn't recall my name.

It was a statement of fact uttered without apology or remorse. When a prompt reply was not forthcoming, she slumped off to the bedroom without saying good night.

I sat by the fire for at least an hour, pondering our plight. The disease was progressing faster than the doctor had predicted. Forty-five years of giving orders as a Colonel in the Marines did nothing to prepare or qualify me to handle her condition. All I could think about was the pact we made years earlier that we would always take care of each other, no matter what. We even wrote it down and signed at the bottom of the page. Of course, a written document wasn't really necessary. We just did that on a whim, perhaps to prove to each other that we were serious and fully committed. Document or not, I would have never abandoned her or put her in a nursing home, not when she needed me the most. Nobody would ever take care of my Edie other than me. I just had to figure out how I was going to hold up my end of the bargain.

After checking up on her, I straggled down the road through the late-night mist. On an impulse, I drifted into the market on the corner and bought my first pack of cigarettes. The ones with a red bullseye on the package. Can't recall the name of the brand, some vague reference to good luck.

Both of my parents smoked. A cigarette hung out of mom's mouth most of the time, but dad only smoked when deep in thought or burdened by an overwhelming problem. It struck me that perhaps that might work for me too. I'd only taken one puff on a cigarette in my entire life, and that didn't go well. I gagged and choked so much that I vowed to never smoke again. And I didn't, until the day of my 85th birthday. The day my wife forgot who I was.

The doorbell interrupted my reminiscing. A polite knock followed, telling me that it wasn't the wise guy process server. So, I trudged into the house. When I opened the front door, I found enough lasagna to feed a high school football team, along with a note from Mrs. Clark across the street apologizing for running off. She was late for her hair appointment. She knew lasagna was my favorite and had been leaving me a batch every week since Edie's passing. A few days later, Mrs. Bradford baked me a chocolate cake. I was no longer so fond of sweets though; traded them in for cigarettes a few years ago. But I appreciated the thoughtfulness. She stayed and talked for a spell, but my eyelids grew heavy half-way through her story about some vacation she'd been on with her husband and grandkids. I gave most of the cake to the dog next door.

Mark and Julie stopped by from time to time after the funeral, usually unannounced. I didn't like that; they oft times caught me off guard and at my worst. But I hadn't heard from them since the Notice of Mark's Application for Guardianship was served.

The only other person that came to the house was Billy, the kid down the street. Every Saturday he mowed the lawn, pulled weeds, raked leaves, and did whatever else was needed in the yard. Took him a few hours. I'd leave him a nice $20 bill under the doormat every week. Thought I was being generous until I read the note he left under the mat one day stating that his rate had gone up to $30. I complied; sure didn't want to do all that work myself. A few weeks later I began feeling guilty about perhaps underpaying him all that time. So, I started leaving two $20 bills under the mat each week. That assuaged my guilt, but it wasn't enough to retain his services. Soon thereafter he left a note informing me that he was going off to college and couldn't work for me anymore. Didn't know what I was going to do about the yard.

The slow trickle of visitors dwindled to an occasional drip in the month or so after being served. Spacing between showers expanded to days at a time and I didn't bother shaving often. Certainly no need to get out of my pajamas on cold days. Daily walks turned into a stroll to the mailbox. I always loved to read, but now found myself falling asleep in the middle of chapters. I seemed to have lost my appetite and missed meals regularly. I felt myself slipping more and more into hermit-hood. But most disturbing, I didn't seem to have any strong desire to climb out.

Julie called one day and asked if they could visit. She said Mark wanted to talk things out and see if our issues could be resolved without lawyers. I told her that I'd cook dinner for them. But I thought to myself, *they didn't need a lawyer, but they'll have to hire an army if they wanted to shove me out of my house.*

They arrived mid-afternoon the following Sunday. Mark flapped his hand in the air. "Please open some windows, Julie."

I said, "It was a long drive just to nag me about my smoking, Mark."

Julie didn't even flinch towards the window. "And it'll be an even longer drive home. Cut the drama, Mark." She tossed him a look that every man dreads receiving from his wife while she zipped her index finger across her throat.

We sat down for dinner and Mark spoke first. "Your yard looks horrible, Pop. The grass hasn't been cut for weeks."

Julie added, "Your neighbors must be aghast. Have they not complained?" It seemed there was a not-so-sweet side to sweet Julie.

Mark resumed. "Dad, the real reason for our visit is that we would very much like you to consider moving closer to us. We love you and would like to see you more. But we are so busy with our jobs, kids, and grandkids, it's hard to visit with you so far away. So, what do you say, Pop?"

"I've lived in this house most of my life," I said. "And I've got no plans to move, now or ever."

"Look, Pop. We all get old and aren't as sharp as we used to be. Someday I'll be in your shoes," Mark said. "But for now, I feel responsible for your well-being."

"I can darn well take care of myself. Besides, where would you propose that I live? With you and Julie?" I said. I tried to contain my amusement. I knew Mark wouldn't like that, but it was good to see him squirm a bit. "I don't think I could live with a Smoke-A-Phobic."

"Well, that probably wouldn't be best for you, Pop. There's so much commotion with the grandkids always coming by, and the noise from their music and friends. You know how it is."

I didn't reply. I enjoyed watching Mark fidget some.

"We think if you would visit Sunshine Manor, you would like and appreciate the facility," Mark said. "They offer a nice two-room apartment with a bedroom and small living room. There are other people to socialize with. And there is always someone there to help if you need it."

Julie chimed in, "You've lost weight and your color isn't good. The excellent food at the Manor should bring you right back to life."

I smiled, but was at a loss for an appropriate retort. Perhaps the sweet side of Julie was an illusion from the beginning.

Mark added, "The nursing staff is on duty 24 hours per day and the ER is only five minutes away." I noted a tiny uptick in the corners of his mouth as he uttered 'ER.'

"It's one of the top-rated assisted care facilities in the state," Julie said. "All we ask is that you consider it. Pay them a visit; we'll come pick you up."

"You'll be pleased to know that I'm a step ahead of you," I said. "In anticipation of this topic arising, I have given serious deliberation to Sunshine Manor and spent a considerable amount of time researching the facility online."

"Splendid," Mark blurted. "We're delighted."

"When the website didn't answer all my questions, I called them. Had a nice talk with the Head Supervisor, Mrs. Blake, I believe."

"That's exciting. How did you like it?" Julie asked

"Mrs. Blake was very pleasant. And the facility seems top notch. Regrettably, I find myself unable to reside at the Sunshine Manor."

"Oh, for heaven's sake, why not?" Mark exclaimed.

"Sunshine Manor is a smoke free facility," I said.

They departed before I had a chance to serve dessert. Pity, I made a special trip to the bakery to buy blueberry cheesecake, Julie's favorite. The dog next door was in for another treat.

* * * * * * *

I stewed the next few days; emotions roller-coastered from hurt feelings to anger to "who cares" to "screw you" back to hurt feelings. The dial finally stopped at "NO," *No, no, no. I do not accept their edict. I'll fight back, that's what I'll do. They'll not stick me in that smoke-free nursing home. I'm the captain of my life, not Mark or anybody else.* I called the next morning and scheduled my psychological examination with Dr. Carol Maloney.

I arrived at Dr. Maloney's office the following Friday half an hour early, clean shaven and freshly showered. She was friendly, perhaps a bit too chummy. She insisted that I call her Carol.

Carol reeled me in with a string of easy questions, name, address, my favorite baseball team, and who I thought would win the Super

Bowl. Carol Maloney was calm, subtle in her movements, mild in her manner of speech, and smiled with sincere interest at every question. She reached for a notepad, picked up a pen, and ratcheted it up a bit; getting a little more personal. "What do you do for entertainment?" "Do you ever go to the movies or the theatre?" "How do you get along with your neighbors?" She noted my hesitation and jotted a few notes. "How often do you get out of the house?" "Are you eating well?" I stuttered a bit and she scribbled some more.

Then Dr. Maloney charged in for the kill. "How many cigarettes are you smoking each day?" I stammered that I didn't keep track. "Are you showering and shaving every day?" I mumbled that I shower whenever necessary. "Once a week, twice a week?" I tried to regain the upper hand with strength and confidence. I noted that cowboys in the Old West only bathed a few times per year. I knew at once that this was not a judicious remark. But like an ill-advised email, it was irretrievable upon smacking the send button. A slight smirk appeared on her face, but she didn't comment. "Did you have your electricity turned off for a few days last month?" I wondered how she knew about that. I explained that the electric company may have forgotten to send my bill, or perhaps it got misplaced amidst all the junk mail. "Really, three months in a row?" I offered a shrug, but she didn't seem satisfied. She asked if I'd had my driver's license all over town. I explained that I had another appointment next week with DMV to re-take my eye test. I expected her to write that down. She didn't. She asked if I had driven to her office that day. I didn't answer. Dr. Maloney then propelled an eight-by-ten photograph gliding across the table, coming to a stop right in front of me. Before looking at the photo, I wondered how many times she had practiced that maneuver to attain the maximum affect. I glanced down and knew at once that my day could not be salvaged. It was a picture of my ramshackle front yard, grass over a month long. Weeds cloaked whatever flowers may or may not have existed. Piles of leaves lingered from the last wind or two, and a large branch from my pepper tree rested atop a broken fence. "Has the appearance of your yard improved since this picture was taken?" I shook my head; there was no good answer.

* * * * * * *

 I slumped out of the office of Dr. Carol Maloney, knowing I had failed her psychological examination. I supposed Mark had probably already received the news and was reserving my spot in the Sunshine Manor at that very moment. I drove home and chain smoked the rest of the day. I was on my third Jack Daniels double when the doorbell rang; followed by a soft knock. Mrs. Clark stood at the door with a casserole pan of lasagna in hand. "May I join you for dinner?" I invited her in, happy for the company and the lasagna.

 We talked about Italian recipes, the weather, and our dead spouses. On my second helping of lasagna, Mrs. Clark asked, "Do you have any plans for your yard?"

 I shuddered, embarrassed that the topic had been mentioned. "The condition of the garden should improve soon," I said. "I'll be selling the house and moving into the Sunshine Manor."

 I think she noted my disheartened demeanor. "I'm relatively new to the neighborhood," she said. "But you've lived here a long time. Do you mind telling me why you are moving?"

 "My son had been pressuring me to move into an assisted-care facility ever since Edie passed," I said. "Mark filed a guardianship application to force the issue. And I flunked the psychological examination this morning."

Mrs. Clark, Connie at her insistence, replied, "I certainly hope you will not cave in to this nonsense." Her feisty attitude made me wonder if she had experienced a similar predicament.

"I despise the thought of moving to that nursing home. Yet I fear that I'll be forced to do so. I haven't slept since my son stepped in to ruin my life."

"We may be old, but we're still alive. And our lives belong to us, not to them," she said. "You've got a sound mind and you must stand up for your rights and fight." Her rhetoric took me back to the old days of inspiring my troops before combat.

"My sentiments exactly. But I really struck out in the psych exam. I barged into her office on a crusade, and limped out a humbled man. The judge places an extraordinary amount of weight on the psychiatrist's recommendation."

Connie reached across the table and placed both her hands atop mine. "It's not too late. We need to formulate a strategy. When is the hearing scheduled?" Her confidence reignited my optimism.

"The hearing is three weeks from today. What do you suggest?" I replied.

"We've got plenty of time, but we need to get hopping," she said. I saw my younger self in the mirror and was pleased to have her on my side. "First of all, Billy's younger brother Ricky is looking for work. I'll call him tonight about getting your yard in order."

"That's good," I said. "I'll contact my CPA; have him send his bookkeeper out to help pay my bills on time and keep the money straight." I poured us both another glass of wine. Nothing got my juices flowing more than sitting around the table formulating a battle plan.

"Last, and most importantly, we need to

get you a job," Connie said. "If you are gainfully employed, the judge will flush Mark's application right down the toilet."

"I don't mind working. But there aren't many job openings for a man my age."

"My grandson, George, is the manager at the local McDonalds. I'll have him call you this weekend to schedule an interview."

"Ha, McDonalds," I slapped my hand on the table. "That'll rankle that meddlesome son of mine."

I arose and scooted around the table. She stood up. I gave Mrs. Connie Clark a big hug and kissed her square on the lips. "Thank you." Hard to lose with General Patton on your side.

* * * * * *

Billy came by the next morning, his brother Ricky in tow. Billy sang his sibling's praises and Ricky assured me that he would do the same good job Billy did. But he wanted to start with two $20 bills each Saturday. I hired Ricky; no squabbling over the price. I promised to pay him extra to get things caught up. He started that day.

George set up my interview Monday morning with his assistant manager, Maria. I hadn't been on a job interview in nearly 70 years, but I wasn't nervous. I had the feeling that the path to employment would be mine for the asking. Mrs. Clark was a hard woman to say no to. I had a friendly chat with Maria and answered all her questions. She said I was the oldest applicant they ever had. Maria hired me on the spot. We didn't discuss compensation; I didn't care. I would be back in my rocking chair in a few weeks.

The next day, I showed up early for my first four-hour shift at the McDonalds on Third Street. Maria assigned Lissette to show me around. She provided instruction and answered my questions. It felt a bit awkward reporting to a girl who looked like she was still in high school plowing through the late stages of puberty, but I didn't mind. How hard could a job like this be? I just needed to see my way through the next few weeks and regain my freedom. Lissette emphasized that smoking was prohibited, even on breaks. I could manage to abstain for four hours.

Lissette placed me on clean up duty the first few days. I cleared tables, re-stocked the condiments, kept the floors clean, and smiled at the customers. My hourly rate was less than Ricky's, but the work was easier. The kids made a mess, especially the toddlers, but the restaurant was small and easy to keep clean. I enjoyed working out front with the customers. I hadn't smiled and said hello so many times in a day for decades, probably in my entire life. It seemed that a smile generally elicited a smile in return, was rarely ignored, and never evoked a scowl. I chatted with customers, fetched drinks and condiments for them, and caught myself whistling as I scurried about. When Lissette admired my whistling, I thought of my mom. She always said that only happy people whistle while they work. I'd always pooh-poohed that saying. Now I had reconsidered.

One day a little boy of about eight or so spilled ketchup all over the front of his shirt. His mother gave him a severe scolding to the point of bringing the boy to tears. I offered to try to remove the stain, but the mother insisted that there was no point, the shirt was ruined. "Well then, there's no downside to letting me give it a whirl." The boy recognized the slight prospect for reprieve. He ripped off his shirt and handed it to me. The mother shook her head, but offered her reluctant consent by flapping her hand at the wrist, much like Mark waves at my cigarette smoke. I took the shirt to the back and got to work on the garment for about fifteen minutes.

When I returned the shirt, the mother was appreciative, and I was the boy's favorite super-hero for the day. Maria tossed me a thumbs up from across the room.

Over the next few weeks I worked the register, assembled Big Macs, tossed salad and did whatever else Lissette asked me to do. She kept me out front most of the time. Lissette knew I relished interacting with the customers. Most of the crew were good to work with. Todd toiled in the kitchen and carried a full load at the local JC. Jose worked the drive thru window. Karen, the other senior citizen, 20 years my junior, lived with her twin sister and accepted no task other than the register. Lissette always seemed to have boyfriend problems, but never let it affect her pleasant demeanor at work. Jack was an ass. Hopefully he would get fired soon. Maria gave me the day off for my hearing.

* * * * * * *

I'm thankful Edie didn't have to see me sitting in a courtroom at a table opposite our only son, daughter-in-law, and their lawyer. Much of the family sat in the gallery. I settled at the table across the room with my attorney, Charlie Richards. Charlie was an old buddy from my days in the Marines, best JAG lawyer I knew. He was not much younger than me and had been retired for years. But he didn't hesitate for a second when I asked him to help me out.

In his opening statement, Mark's attorney buttered up the judge by telling him how much Mark loved his father and had only his well-being and best interests in mind. I bristled. How could a stranger possibly know this? Charlie noted my agitation and calmed me down with a pat on my knee and a finger to his lips. The attorney continued, laying out all the reasons why I needed a legal guardian. *Can't handle his finances, eats poorly, lacks good hygiene, yard was in shambles, smokes excessively, needs to be near his family, poor eyesight, drives around town without a license, and can't take care of himself.* At that point, he kept talking and I stopped listening. Desperation set in with every word delivered so convincingly and with such eloquence. Mark's lawyer rattled off my flaws and shortcomings. It struck me just how far I had fallen. Once the proud, confident Colonel who inspired trust, allegiance and admiration from his troops. Now this. I glanced over at Charlie, his facial expression devoid of emotion. All I saw was thinning white hair, sagging skin, liver spots, and a 30-year-old suit and tie. I closed my eyes and prayed that Charlie was somehow still up to the task.

Mark's attorney called Dr. Carol Maloney as their first witness. She left her friendly disposition and phony smile back at the office. The doctor wore an expensive red business suit and focused on the issue of my competence. She poured through every painful detail of my psychological examination, consulting her exam notes for confirmation. Half an hour later Mark's attorney asked for her conclusion. She removed her glasses and stated that, in her professional opinion, I could not properly take care of myself and should reside in an assisted care facility in near proximity to my family members.

The judge asked Charlie, "Do you have any questions for Dr. Maloney?" Charlie remained seated, paused longer than seemed necessary, then asked the psychiatrist if I suffered from Alzheimer's disease or dementia. She answered no, then Charlie dismissed her.

Mark's attorney concluded his case and the judge asked Charlie to proceed with our case. Charlie kept his head down, shuffling through the documents before him. His movements were slow, methodical, and laborious. Had it been anybody else's life at stake other than my own, I might have nodded off. The judge grew restless and prompted him to action. Charlie didn't respond, but with assistance from the edge of the table and his cane, he rose to his feet.

"I have three pieces of evidence," Charlie said. On the judge's bench, he laid out a picture of Ricky mowing the lawn and one taken from the street proving my yard to be in tip-top shape. The judge studied the photos, then instructed the bailiff to show the pictures to Mark and his attorney.

Charlie retreated to his desk, then hobbled back to the bench. He handed the judge a letter from Martin & Myers, CPAs, stating that they had been employed to send a bookkeeper to my house twice per month to pay my bills, deposit checks, and reconcile my bank account. The letter went on to state that my finances were in excellent condition.

Last, Charlie presented the judge a copy of my McDonalds pay stub along with a letter from the manager, George Clark. The letter stated that I was a valuable employee who worked at least four days per week. My eye caught Julie tapping Mark's arm and emphasizing some part of the McDonalds letter to him.

Charlie offered no exposition with the documents. The judge offered no insight as to the effect the evidence had on him. The smile on the face of Mark's attorney announced his belief that our evidence wasn't enough to sway the judge. I couldn't eradicate the young attorney's words and the testimony of Dr. Carol Maloney from my mind.

Charlie said, "We would like to call Connie Clark as our first witness." I turned to Charlie, but he ignored my query. We hadn't discussed witnesses. He contended the evidence would be sufficient. Charlie charted his own path, and I had no choice but to trust my old friend.

After the usual introductions identifying

Mrs. Clark as my across the street neighbor, Charlie asked her assessment of the portrayal painted by Dr. Maloney and Mark's attorney.

Connie replied, "I wouldn't dispute their conclusions. But they have not told the entire story." She went on to explain in detail that after Edie's passing I lapsed into a month's long depression. "He not only lost his spouse; he lost his purpose in life. It's a mighty blow to the human spirit when you are no longer needed, and your life loses its relevance." She paused and glanced my way, then continued. "Mark's guardianship application demoralized him. Ironically, it was the jolt that brought him back to life. Since that time, he's corrected each item on Dr. Maloney's list and is now leading a rich, satisfying life."

Mark's attorney rose to cross exam Mrs. Clark, but Julie motioned him to sit down. She whispered into Mark's ear for a full minute, perhaps two. Mark nodded his head, but did not speak.

Finally, Mark stood. He looked shaken. I think he was welling up a bit. He stated that he would like to withdraw his application. Perhaps my initial conclusion about sweet Julie was correct after all.

Judge pounded his gavel. "Case dismissed."

On Monday morning I strode into the McDonalds on Third Street and quit my job.

* * * * * * *

Mark and Julie visited me a few days later. The following Sunday, Mark and Julie joined Connie and me for a lasagna dinner. We laughed like in the old days and Mark never once mentioned my cigarettes or waved at my smoke.

Several days passed without another visitor or even a phone call. The days turned to weeks and the weeks to a month. I missed more than a few meals here and there and I couldn't attest to showering and shaving every day. Loneliness crept back into my life.

Julie came by one day and we strolled down to the McDonalds on Third Street for lunch. It was my first time back. The whole gang was there, Maria, Lissette, Todd, Jose, Karen. Everyone except Jack; he'd been fired for cursing at a customer. Good riddance. They were all happy to see me and wished me well, but they had jobs to do. As they retreated to their duties, I felt myself choking up a bit. I missed them more than I'd expected. It occurred to me that my happiest days since Edie passed were my few weeks at McDonalds. I liked my new friends, enjoyed the customers and reveled in being a useful member of a team.

George Clark sat down at our table. He said they all missed me and were disappointed that I had left. I glanced at Julie. She smiled and nodded her head. She knew what I was thinking.

I told George I missed everyone, too. Then I asked him if there was any chance of getting my job back. He grinned and told me I was one the best workers they had.

I reported for work the next morning. It felt good to be needed again

WORDS I STILL CAN'T SAY

by Carly Mastroni

Momma

My first word isn't a word at all. It's nonsense that shrieks from my lips as my proud parents hover above my highchair, fresh-faced and doe-eyed, trying to coax me into repeating it. My mom holds an enormous video camera in front of my face, wanting to save the memory forever. My dimples show as I knock around my smashed peaches. It doesn't matter that my word isn't a real word, it only matters that it isn't "Momma" or "Dada" like they wanted. They're not worried. They have no reason to be.

"It's my name!" My four-year-old sister squeals. I repeat it at the sound of her voice.

She runs to tickle me, and I say it a third time, "Lala." The name rolls off my tongue, high pitched and overexcited.

My parents don't care that my sister's name is "Alex," and that I've switched the L and the A to create an entirely new word. They don't see any need for concern. For months, they coo their names as they kiss my chubby cheeks and bribe me with sweets, but I don't speak their words. They begin to worry. Gibberish is my first language, and I learn it all too well. I forget what my mom looks like without worry lines, but I remember the Georgia O'Keeffe red poppy painting hanging on the wall behind her head.

Carly

I decide my name is Abby in the produce aisle of a Jewel Osco. The stalks of celery my mother throws into the squeaking cart are no longer than my legs, but I'm already embarrassed to need an interpreter to translate my name. Alex, whose head barely reaches the handle, pushes the cart forward. I sit facing her. She sticks her tongue out at me. It's blue from a Baby Bottle Pop, and I mirror her with my red tongue until we erupt in a burst of giggles too loud for the ladies shopping for vegetables to ignore.

"They're adorable," a woman says to my mom as she compares avocados.

"Oh, thank you."

The woman waves to me and coos, "Hi sweetheart," before turning back to my mom and switching to her normal voice when she asks, "What are their names?"

My sister hops on the cart, ready to put herself front and center so I can disappear into the silent background I prefer. "I'm Alex, and this is my little sister Carly."

"Abby," I correct.

I see my mom sigh, her frail shoulders slumping over, but she doesn't argue. She lets the woman think this is normal toddler behavior and not a disability she'll have to explain to a stranger. She thinks this is my brain's newest way of pronouncing "Carly." Maybe it is. Maybe it isn't a decision, but a mistake. Maybe my mind needs a name it won't be embarrassed to say, so it changed the pronunciation the way it does with every other word. Maybe I have no control, but I want to pretend I do.

Abby is an easy word, the kind my mouth can form, and my brain cannot confuse. Ah-bee. I can say it without fumbling. Nobody will look to my mom for help when they can't decipher it on their own, and then ask my sister when even my mom can't figure out what I've said. They won't have to ask twice or nod to hide the discomfort of not understanding. My mom lugs a watermelon into the cart, and I wonder if the new me with the new name will still hate the taste and texture of it on my tongue.

Squirrel

A bunny runs up the tree outside the window that I can't stop looking through and stashes acorns in whatever hole it can find. I know it's not a bunny, but I'd rather sound dumb than incoherent. When the man from the seven o'clock news asks what I'm looking at, I don't try to pronounce the bushy-tailed animal's name. I say the wrong word on purpose, but I say it the right way, and the man with the mustache behind the camera smirks at the mistake he thinks I've made.

I play with my Spice Girls crew neck and answer the newsman's questions about cluttering, apraxia, and mixed speech sound disorder. He wants to know about the Fis phenomenon, but I want to be off camera. There are too many people behind its lens. I can see their eyes in the reflection of my own, watching, waiting to pity the little girl on their screens.

This interview is supposed to be a heartwarming CBS Chicago special on children overcoming obstacles, but it feels like a betrayal. My parents aren't here. Alex isn't here to translate. I sit alone at a table with a handful of other students in my elementary school that, like me, also have obstacles that need overcoming. Their faces blur in my mind, their names I forget, but in our chairs sit our disabilities: deaf, blind, autistic, dyslexic, ADHD, and speech disorder. These are our names now, our identities.

When I came home with a permission slip in my worn green folder two weeks ago, my father signed it without reading it, without telling my mom or sister. He was too drunk to bother, just like he is too drunk to work, to cook, to pick me up from speech lessons. He is always too drunk, his jaw always covered in a five o'clock shadow, his eyes always slumped with bags slouching onto his cheeks.

I would rather be sitting at a desk reading The Giver instead of in this room trying to pretend I am happy and prospering for thousands of viewers to see. With a too-white smile and a too-orange tan, the newsman admires my bravery as I doodle vines on my folder. I draw myself stuck in them, dangling upside-down. I don't think talking is an act of courage, but I don't tell him this. I nod and practice saying, "Thank you" over and over in my head.

Accent

The new girl in the bedazzled Limited Too t-shirt asks me where I'm from as we ride the school bus home.   The conversation I'm having with my neighbor about my parents' fighting comes to a halt at the new girl's question. The bus goes over a bump, and my backpack falls forward. I pick it up along with some spilled gel pens, hoping she will drop it and assume I didn't hear her, but my hopes fall somewhere beneath the seats in front of me.

She wants to know what my accent is and starts taking guesses when I do not respond, "British? Scottish?" My neighbor doesn't know what to say, so she says nothing. The new girl keeps taking guesses, "South African?"

"She's from here. We're literally pulling up to the house we've lived in our entire lives," Alex answers for me. She sits diagonally from my seat, far enough away to talk to her friends, but close enough to overhear if I need her.

The last two minutes of our bus ride move slowly, every stop sign taking up years of my life. I stay silent for those years.

Rolo

The dark room at the end of the school's hallway is the most comforting place I know. For thirteen years, I've spent Mondays, Wednesdays, and Fridays in the speech therapist's office. Mrs. Johnson has sour gummy worms and Rolo's in the top right drawer of her desk. I'm allowed to open it and eat as many as I want as long as I'm talking. She says she doesn't care what I say. She just wants me to have the confidence to keep talking.

With wrinkled hands, she holds up a white curved pipe. I hold it up like a phone, my muscle memory taking over. She tells me to speak into it. She doesn't have to. I know the drill.

"Cookie."

This exercise is part of my specific speech disorder therapy. My mind isn't capable of hearing how I actually sound. First, my brain sends down the wrong sounds to my mouth, then my mouth can't pronounce them properly, and lastly, my ears hear everything as if I am saying it all correctly. It comes out as nonsense that no one except my sister can decipher. Even my mom admits that sometimes she nods and pretends to understand after she's had a long day and doesn't have the energy to decode my verbal hieroglyphics. Mrs. Johnson has tried having me watch myself in videos and listening to recordings of my voice, but nothing helps it register. My brain still thinks it hears the words I say exactly as I say them.

"Say it again."

I repeat it another time, expecting to hear "cookie" like always. The word echoes up into my ears and travels through the auditory nerve for my brain to declare it as a specific sound. Usually, this last step is where it struggles, but for the first time, my mind hears what I've said. It clicks.

I pronounced it, "Woolie."

"Now try again," Mrs. Johnson says in a monotone voice. This activity is routine, something we often do with little result. I think she stopped hoping a while ago. She toys with her pearl earring, hung below her short, peppered hair, and I wonder if she thinks of me as a student or a grandchild. Probably a mixture of the two.

"Coolie."

My eyes must give me away, or maybe this is my first correction. I'm not sure if I've ever actually corrected a word until today. Mrs.

Johnson eyebrows shoot up, and she tries to hide her smile.

"Cookie."

She puts the pipe back in a cardboard box and hugs me tight. We've been together since my first day of preschool, and now I'm about to start high school. We know this is the beginning of the end of our time together. I'm almost fixed.

Chatterbox

My mom takes me out to celebrate when my chemistry teacher calls home to complain that I'm talking too much in class. He calls me a disruptive chatterbox. I wish more than anything that I could have heard the conversation, listened to his reaction when my mother thanked him and told him how happy she was to hear that I've been behaving this way.

I lived my life without a comprehensible language for so long, screaming through a broken radio, that when I finally found the right connection, I talked until my throat burned. I told everyone everything about me, in every detail, using every adjective I could think of, said every word of every story I ever wanted to tell. I became a girl who loved to be at the center of attention. I moved and positioned a spotlight until it focused solely on my mouth and then turned the volume on the microphone up until the floor rattled beneath my feet.

Sitting in a booth at my favorite Thai restaurant, my mother twists the ghost of an absent wedding band, and the artificial lighting hollows her already sharp cheekbones. She doesn't cook. My father was the one who did that, which means by the end, we went hungry most nights when she worked late. The waitress comes over to ask if we're ready. Alex orders a spicy salmon roll. She's gotten quieter as I've gotten louder. There's no need for her to be my translator, my protector, or even my second parent like she was right after our dad left. She doesn't know what role to fill. I want her to be my sister, but that's a role she's never gotten to fully play, and I don't think she's comfortable in it. I order my meal by myself—pad see ew with beef—and for the first time, I know the waitress understands what I'm saying.

Worm/Warm

I sip on a red solo cup with lukewarm beer in an attempt to distract myself from my high school friend's commands. I wonder absently how my father chose this over a family. It tastes god awful, but it's better than the taste of the words on my lips. I've become a party trick. My speech disorder is no better than crushing a beer can on my forehead.

"Say worm," Alexis says.

I shake my head and take another swig. Alexis flips her long blonde hair over her shoulder and smiles at me. We were friends before I could speak, which means she's allowed to mess with me about it. It's the people around us, the ones that wouldn't have bothered trying to talk to me before, that make me nervous. They're football players, basketball stars, and cheerleaders, and I'm amazed to think of how the titles that sit around me have changed in only a few years.

"Please, come on. How about warm?" Alexis pleads.

They all tell me to say the words, the ones I can't distinguish between, so I think of other words instead. A squiggly insect in the ground. A slimy bug drowned out by rain. Mild, temperate, nice. Good weather. I think of moving to Antarctica. I would never have to say either word if I lived there. I don't think worms can dig through ice, and warm would never be a topic of discussion.

"Werm," I say, mispronouncing it as severely as I can on purpose to make it a joke that I'm in on rather than one I'm not. My friends laugh, we drink, the night moves on, but I can't.

No matter how far I've come, no matter what words I've trained myself to say, there are still so many that my mouth can't form correctly. Worm and warm are too similar, and it is too difficult to distinguish between them. Even my brain can't tell which one it's trying to say. "R's" have always been my kryptonite, and I hate that there is no language I can learn that doesn't include them in their alphabet. I work my way around these words. I say hot instead of warm, I say bug instead of worm. I think maybe I should research that college in Antarctica.

Pint

It takes nineteen years for someone to correct me. It's too late to change. My brain and my mouth are not connected, these two are not friends, and they will not listen to one another. I thought I was fixed. I practiced in front of mirrors and into curved pipes to force my brain to watch and listen to what my mouth has to say. I sunk into my mom's bed surrounded by expensive paintings and studied the signatures of artists whose names I fought to say. I read dictionaries out loud, memorizing the taste of each syllable on my tongue until I thought they were impossible to mispronounce. It's too late to tell my brain I got one wrong.

My college friends start pronouncing "pint" the way I do so that it rhymes with "mint" instead of "night." Yes, "night" is a slant rhyme, but as it turns out very little rhymes with the correct pronunciation of pint. They mean it as a joke. They have never heard a version of me that couldn't speak properly. They didn't grow up with me, didn't have to watch me struggle to say my own name.

I don't tell them any differently. Instead, I stop buying comfort food in small sizes. A gallon of ice cream takes up too much room in my freezer and puts too much weight on my hips, but I buy

the gallon anyway and tell the checkout girl it's
been a long week.

Drunk

My friends think it's funny that I go mute
when I'm drunk. I reach for another hard
lemonade from a cooler filled with melted
ice in an attempt to distract myself from their
conversations. I go mute when I get put on the
spot. I go mute when I'm nervous, when I'm
flustered, when I'm happy, sad, or excited. I go
mute because I need control. I need to think
about the words I'm going to say, picture their
letters in my mind, read the syllables one by one
as they light up like a karaoke machine inside my
eyelids.
They call to me, "Hello, Carly? Did you go mute?"
"She could be an excellent mime."
"Or monk," they decide.
It's the only way I can talk and be sure I
won't make a mistake. They think it's just a drunk
characteristic. They don't know that I lived inside
my head for so long that it feels natural like
maybe it's the only way I know to exist.

Anesthesia

My college roommates and I sit around
watching one of our parent's Netflix accounts
because we can't afford cable. One is terrified
because she's going to have to get her tonsils
taken out, and the doctor told her it's a much
worse procedure as an adult.
"You'll be under anastasia for the worst of
it, and then they'll give you plenty of pain meds.
Plus, we'll take care of you, and your mom's
going to come up to visit," I say.
Two of the girls let it slide. They heard the
mistake, but they have enough empathy to
ignore it. Unfortunately, I have three roommates,
and one does not have a filter.
"Anastasia? Like the Russian princess
movie? What are you, an idiot?"

I cringe. This roommate doesn't mean any harm, but her words strike hard and leave a mark. I have a twenty-minute speech to give tomorrow for a Communications final, so I can't let myself get in my head. It'll only make it worse. I chose it as my minor to prove that I could do it, that I could finally communicate with the rest of the world, but there are moments like these, moments that remind me that there is still a disconnect between my ears, my mind, and my mouth. It feels like I'm floating between them, between what I want to say and what I can say, tethered to each one with vines that choke me any time I pull too hard.

I go up to my room early that night, faking a headache. I call Alex. Not because I want to vent or complain, but because I want to talk and talking comes easily with her.

The dial rings once, twice, three times. I wait to hear her recorded voice, the one we spent an afternoon recording before she left for college. We giggled and messed it up about a hundred times before we finally got it right.

The recorded version of her begins, "Hey, it's Alex. I can't talk right now. I'm shoe shopping."

I smile. Just hearing her makes me feel better. "Hey Pal, it's me," I start using a nickname so old I can't remember if it came from a speech issue or an inside joke, "Just calling to say hi and that I miss you. Call me later if you get a chance."

Impediment

I can feel the disconnect growing. My brain becomes a balloon that floats a mile above my jaw, tethered by stretched out nerves caught on my jagged, concrete tongue. It happens when I've slept too much—or not at all, or when I've forgotten to focus—but mainly it happens when there are too many people listening. My words are not the right words, or they are the right words, but they're said the wrong way. Sometimes they're not words at all and sometimes they are my words, but they're jumbled and out of order and sometimes they're mushed together into one big word.

The world does what it's supposed to do; it spins on its axis and revolves around the sun. My mother buys new paintings and orders takeout when I come home. My father, wherever he is, slurs his words more than me. My sister learns how to be my sister instead of my interpreter, and sometimes I miss the bond that only she and I could share. Sometimes I miss when there was only one person who could truly understand me because it created a world of our own. Then sometimes my brain says one thing, and my mouth says another, and in the real world, people don't always know how to deal with defects. I remember how much my heart ached when I wanted to say something articulate and, instead, had to play charades.

I'm not sure which to blame, my mouth, my ears, or my mind, so I don't blame any. I prepare myself for their mistakes and keep talking.

A CERTAIN SLANT OF LIGHT
BY REBECCA RUTH GOULD
SERIES- LODHI GARDENS
(digital photography, 2019)

BOOKS NOT BOMBS BY DANIEL STAUB WEINBERG
SERIES- SEEING IS BELIEVING
(photography 8 x 10 in, 2019)

PORTRAIT OF A WOMAN BY JODIE FILAN
(B&W, acrylic paint & markers 18 x 24 in, 2019)

POETRY
POETRY
POETRY
POETRY
POETRY
POETRY
POETRY
POETRY
POETRY
POETRY
POETRY
POETRY
POETRY
POETRY
POETRY

Tea Time

by BINA RUCHI PERINO

A poem is a memory, steeped in hot water,
a suspended bag of dead things: dried leaves

and crushed herbs for taste. I didn't start drinking
tea until college, and a psychiatrist diagnosed

General Anxiety Disorder. A chicken or the egg
situation; was it nature or nurture? I nurtured
contempt.

I was a bone-framed body of a girl never finishing
her food, always hunched over with stomach pain.

I learned to stare out the car window as Father hit
Mother in the front seat. I've been living through a
window.

My rattled brain: angry, angry, angry. I counted
sidewalk cracks between bus stop and home,
surviving on escape.

Was I just sensitive? Hurricane Katrina never hit Texas,
but I couldn't stop screaming. Father took a broom

to my brother's body on the kitchen floor. I haven't
stopped screaming. I keep steeping the tea. I know
they're not here.

Listen, I know it's in the past. These dead things still
matter. They're giving the hot water a flavor. Not
chamomile or jasmine,

not something nice to swallow. It's the flavor of sense.
I want this pain to make sense.

Autumn Memory

by JOANNE ESSER

for Kaitlin, at age nine

This is the kind of day I want
you to remember when you think back,

a perfect yellow morning, a rustling
of fallen leaves, the smell of soil damp and eager,

a walk to nowhere. I want you
to remember me as the kind of mother

who led you leisurely, longingly
down the sidewalk, who noticed

shapes of gingko and toothed elm,
all the shades of oak gold, maple red,

who held things up to the light
and felt their brittleness,

who collected the best specimens
and ironed them between sheets of wax paper

just for the sake of looking at them longer.

But in truth, it was you who led.
Your bright eyes and slow-paced steps,

you who insisted we lay in the grass under the tree
and look up through red-orange lace,

feel the planet turn under us,
spin us into imagined dizziness.

My long-grown mind kept trying to tug me
away from the wheeling colors,

look at my watch, worry about the coming cold.
You pulled me under the layer of leaves,

sprinkled them on me, burying me
deep enough to remember

my own long-lost familiar girl.

ALONE IS ALONE

by LOUIS P. NAPPEN

Despite the nomenclature:
A "twin" is a single-sized bed.
A "double" or "full" are a twin and a half.
A "queen" is a double plus half a half twin,
and a "king" is the size of two twins.

In England, however, the queen is a king
unless she possesses a "super king"
which, nonetheless, provides
less blanket expanse
than a "California king."

(Think Henry the Eighth
--the size of two twins--
or Princess Grace Kelly
--a "California queen," more or less.)
It's human nature personified

to feel more lonely and cold
if you are royalty or a movie star
(so I've been told). That being said,
I know by experience that
absent a queen (or a king,

if that's your thing) or an actual twin,
alone is alone, and stillness
chills indiscriminately
no matter the glacial acreage
of your misnomered mattress.

SEVERED ROOTS

by Sofia Martimianakis

Our family tree shook in anger
through whirlwinds of betrayal
A brother who took advantage
of his sister's gentle nature, who
turned his back when she
vulnerable and alone, reached out
as leaves reach for the sun
Only to find the first signs of a storm
ambiguous skies of cruel jokes
thunderclaps of arguments
warning of the moment
lightning words
would burn bridges
in generations to come.
A family left searching
for signs of regrowth,
for faint glimmers of unity

Sibling roots cannot be severed
without weakening the entire tree.

WHAT GETS TO ME

by Gwen Hart

Not the flatland, but the wind.
Not the kernel, but the cob.
Not the turbine, but the spin.
Not the cattle, but the prod.

Not the train, but the whistle.
Not the gravel, but the road.
Not the flower, but the thistle.
Not the semi, but the load.

Not the prairie, but the weeds.
Not the lightning, but the bug.
Not the berry, but the seeds.
Not the milk, but the jug.

Not the quilting, but the needle.
Not the dog, but the bark.
Not the dung, but the beetle.
Not the stars, but the dark.

I LEFT NEBRASKA
(a prose poem)

by Stuart Forrest

I will never miss Nebraska's winter. It raids
across that flat land; its icy spears stabbing
through clothes, into the soul of folk
who walk about town; unsteady, swaddled,
waddling black and white penguins;
black and white penguins that hate each other
in the midst of a storm. It snows with anger
in Nebraska; blowing drifts as big as bison,
and the black and white cold lasts all year long.
Life, within the heart, does not thaw in July,
when water steams from concrete
and suspicion is a frozen over slush between people.
I can never go back to the cold. I can never
go back to my first home.

OF GRANDFATHER AND POLLIWOGS

by DEBORA CHAPPEL

You held the hand of the
grandfather you had never known
after the rain left puddles on the patio.

You showed him how to
Stir sand in the puddles so that
pyrite shimmered in the sunlight.

You dragged him further
into the backyard through the
hollyhocks and the four o'clocks.

You told him to sit in the
sandbox and he helped build
sandcastles and fortresses.

You urged him into the secret
space behind the grapevine and
ate the unripe and sour grapes.

You pulled him to the polliwog
pond and showed him the rear legs
and a tear rolled down his face.

He was gone the next morning
and your mom and dad acted
like he'd never been there at all.

AFRAID OF DEATH, WHO ME?

by HANNA FOX

I wonder if I should dip my toes
into the forbidding cold water
as I stand at the edge of the sea
at the Jersey shore mid-winter.

Should I end my life before it ends me
like accomplished women I admire
writer Virginia Woolf, who walked into a river
or feminist Carolyn Heilbrun, who took an
overdose

If only I knew what to expect
since I don't believe in a hereafter
yet I have this recurring fantasy
of us swirling in space forever

invisible weightless drones
able to see what's happening below.
I'd shrug my bodiless shoulders and sigh
Wondering what I was afraid of while alive.

Crows

by Claudia Buckholts

Crows dive-bomb the oak, stir up a ruckus,
a flim-flam of croaks, and sparrows flee,

recalcitrant squirrels escape to roofs. Amid
the melee, I watch disorder grow, a system

barricaded while sunlight effaces the shadows
of afternoon. Crows use what tools they have:

beak, squawk, claw-feet, the instrument of wings.
If humans weren't bound to earth, but ejected

into air, with artificial wings, what skirmishes
we might create, what new rumpus. Instead

we bicker down here, the terrestrial flux like
a soldering iron welds us to the turning planet.

GIBRALTAR ON MY MIND

by Jack Donahue

Ceiling shadows tell the story of a boy
who lives longer than anyone ever lived,
dead or alive.

To his delight, elongated puppets play out
the fantasies of what could have been,
the story of a dance in time
whenever time stands still.

Nightlights turn bedposts on their sides,
morph them into forty-ton cannons
rolled into crenels, taking aim at enemy ships.
The balls are dead, duds never fired
but the rocks in the sea splinter the ships.

Many survivors swim ashore,
wave white flags
seek a lasting peace,
a safe place for family and friends
and hopefully new friends
all floating gracefully on the stage above,
moving freely within a time that does not exist
until the curtain opens unto a brand new day.

TEACHER'S FINAL NOTE

by Jack Donahue

It was the last note she wrote
before taking leave,
more of a mother's plea
devoid of all pedantry,
filled with concern for a boy
enrolled in the wrong school,
every outside door festooned
with the peacockery of blue ribbons,
bragging on the latest test scores.

He needs to be switched to a place
where baby steps are honored
but seldom measured.
More often falling back than jumping ahead,
not every student needs to be told
he will fly like an eagle.

This troubled boy is more of a sparrow:
small, easily overlooked, a personality
dressed each day in camouflage colors,
quite pleased to hop from branch to branch
in search of a limb he can live on,
alongside like minded students of the inner world,
inhabiting the last desk nearest the back door,
out of view, out of range,
desperately scribbling in a notebook
filled with deep, angry strokes,
preliminary sketches drawn
before the masterwork of demonizing failure.

He needs to be taken out
Soon
while he is still a special boy
with special needs,
a child I wish
I could call my own
she wrote in the note
I found years later
in the attic
of her Good Will belongings.

IT WASN'T THE SAME LAKE

by Ray Keifetz

It wasn't the same lake.
The waters we raced across
prows up like rocket ships
never closed over the girl
my mother said she knew,
or read about until she thought she knew,
a lake she'd never seen becoming her lake,
the weight of its mossy waters
pressing the girl deeper into the silt
pressing my mother deeper into herself
until she could no longer tell
one lake from another,
until every lake held
a cold blue girl
as she screamed at me from the shore
unable to tell
one drowning from another.

EDUCATION FOR ALL #5
BY GUILHERME BERGAMINI
(color photography, 2014)

EDUCATION FOR ALL # 9
BY GUILHERME BERGAMINI
(color photography, 2014)

RING TONES
(a play in one act)

by Kip Knott

CHARACTERS:

WIFE: A thirty-something woman with dirty-blonde hair who is dressed in vintage 1940s trousers, blouse, and loafers. She is the spitting image of Lauren Bacall in The Big Sleep.

HUSBAND 1: A thirty-something man with sandy blonde hair and a five-o'clock shadow who is dressed in business casual clothes. He is the spitting image of a thirty-something Justin Timberlake.

HUSBAND 2: A late thirty-something man with jet black hair who is dressed in a dark wool suit with high-waisted trousers. He is the spitting image of Humphrey Bogart in The Big Sleep.

SETTING:

A KITCHEN: The room is furnished with a small, linoleum and chrome table and two matching chairs set center stage. A KITCHEN SINK and small WINDOW are positioned stage left a few feet away from the table. A BOOKSHELF, with some KNICK-KNACKS and an MP3 PLAYER that looks like an antique wooden cathedral radio on the shelves, is positioned center stage a few feet behind the table.

ACT 1
Scene 1

AT RISE: Early evening. The WIFE and HUSBAND 1 sit at the table. The table is set for dinner. A full glass of wine and a half-empty bottle of wine sits in front of HUSBAND 1, and a full glass of wine sits in front of the WIFE.

HUSBAND 1: Can you please turn on some music. You know I can't stand to eat in silence. (Takes a long drink from his wine glass.)

WIFE: Sure.
(Rises lethargically from her chair, shuffles over to the bookshelf, and turns on the MP3 player. "MOONLIGHT SERENADE" by Glenn Miller begins to play. SHE shuffles back over to the table and sits down, refusing to look at HUSBAND 1.)

HUSBAND 1: (Slams his fork down.)
I said music. Music! Like Drake or Bruno Mars. God, even Eminem would be better than this museum soundtrack crap. Change it! I want to hear music.

WIFE: Sure.
(Once again rises lethargically from her chair and shuffles over to the bookshelf and presses a button on the MP3 player. "UPTOWN FUNK" by Bruno Mars begins to play. SHE shuffles back over to the table and sits down, raising her wine glass and smiling a too-big smile at HUSBAND 1.)

HUSBAND 1: Why couldn't you have just played that to begin with?

(They eat a few bites silently.)

WIFE: So did you get your sales report submitted?

HUSBAND 1: No. When Jackson and I got back from lunch Mr. Addison was already gone for the day. So we both said to hell with it, and went to Happy Hour for the rest of the day.

WIFE: Sounds like a productive day.

HUSBAND 1: I'm guessing more productive than yours. Let me guess: You spent your day sitting in your vintage, overstuffed chair perusing auction sites for antiques.

WIFE: You couldn't be more wrong.

HUSBAND 1: Really? Enlighten me.

WIFE: Actually, I sat right here at the kitchen table and perused auctions sites for antiques.

HUSBAND 1: Well, aren't you quite the Little Miss Rebel.
(Empties his wine glass and refills it from the bottle in front of him.)
Did you at least find anything you can make a buck on?

WIFE: I bought a wonderful etching. Grant Wood. 1937. It's real, I think. The seller just listed it as a print. If it's real, it's a three-thousand-dollar piece.

HUSBAND 1: And if it's not real?

WIFE: Then it's a one-hundred-dollar piece.

HUSBAND 1: And how much did you pay?

WIFE: (Takes a slow drink from her wine glass and then looks down at the table.)
Seventy-five dollars. Plus shipping.

HUSBAND 1: Plus shipping. How much was shipping?

WIFE: Twenty dollars.

HUSBAND 1: (Sarcastically)
Five-dollar profit. Nice. Sounds like you had a productive day.

WIFE: But I'm pretty sure it's real. I know I can sell it fast. So it should be a $2,905 profit.

HUSBAND 1: You always say, "I can sell it fast." Have you looked around here lately?

WIFE: (Looks around the kitchen.)
What about it?

HUSBAND 1: What about it? What about it! We're surrounded by the past! That's what! Old dishes, old furniture, and old curtains. The MP3 player looks like an old-fashioned radio. Even the damn house is old!

WIFE: You said you trusted me to find us a house that we could both live in.

HUSBAND 1: I said I wanted something fresh! Something new! Something modern!

WIFE: (Annoyed)
This is the most modern house we looked at. It was built in 1940, for God's sake. It's not old. It's classic.

HUSBAND 1: Oh, well, excuse me! I'm sorry! My mistake! It is positively modern! State of the art! Do you even remember me saying that a condo might be nice?

WIFE: Condo? I never heard you say condo.

HUSBAND 1: Because you never hear what you don't want to hear. When I say play music, you play crap my Grandma wouldn't even like. When I say condo, you hear museum!

(The WIFE picks up her glass for another drink and spills some wine down the front of her blouse.)

HUSBAND 1: (Laughing)
And on top of everything else, I think you have a drinking problem!

WIFE: (Gets up and runs over to the sink where she turns on the water, soaks a dish towel, and begins to wipe off her blouse.)
That's not funny. This is a vintage 1943 Yves St. Laurent blouse.

HUSBAND 1: That's a laugh! Everything about you is vintage! I can't say for sure, but I suspect that you even keep one foot on the floor when we make love! Why do you always have to live in the past, to look back. Backwards, you're backwards.

WIFE : (As SHE furiously scrubs her blouse over the sink, her wedding ring slips off her finger and falls down the drain)
My ring! No! God, no! Not my ring!

(Tries to fish her ring out of the drain with her fingers, then with a butter knife that is lying in the sink)
No, no, no, no!

(Shoulders slump. SHE splashes some water on her face to prepare herself before she turns to tell)

HUSBAND 1: what has happened.

WIFE: Honey, I'm so sorry, but my ring...
(As SHE turns around, she sees that HUSBAND 1's place at the table is empty.)
Honey? Sweetheart?

(Looks around the room, then under the table,

then exits the stage. We hear her calling for HUSBAND 1 offstage.)

Honey? Where are you? Sweetheart? Where'd you go? Sweetie? I'm sorry, honey! I'll ask for a refund on the etching! I'll get our money back! I promise! Honey? Hun?

(Re-enters the kitchen and walks over to HUSBAND 1's place at the table for a closer inspection. Everything at the table is exactly as it was. HUSBAND 1's napkin is draped over the seat of his chair as if he just disappeared. SHE looks around the kitchen totally befuddled. SHE reaches to play with her wedding ring, something she does when she thinks, and remembers that it has fallen down the drain. SHE looks closely at her hand, then at HUSBAND 1's empty chair. SHE walks over to the sink, looks down the drain, then opens the cupboard below and pulls out a toolbox. SHE takes a wrench from the toolbox and begins to dismantle the drainpipe.)

WIFE: Please, God, let me find the ring. If you let me find the ring, I promise I will be a better wife for my husband. Please, please, please.
(Pulls the drainpipe off and reaches in with her fingers.)
Yes! I got it! Yes, yes, yes!

(Rubs the ring on her blouse and slides it back on her finger. SHE takes a deep breath, carefully stands up, and slowly turns around to face the kitchen table. Sitting in HUSBAND 1's chair is a man who is not her husband. He is holding an empty whiskey glass and looks as if he stepped right out of a 1940s detective movie.)

HUSBAND 2: Is everything alright, Dollface?

WIFE: (Rubs her eyes, blinks a few times, and

stares at HUSBAND 2)
Uh … I … uh … who…

HUSBAND 2: What is it, Angel? Why are you
acting all daffy?

WIFE: (Thinks about what to do next, and plays
with the wedding band on her finger. SHE
suddenly lifts her hand up to her face and
inspects the ring closely.)
My ring. No. Not my ring. Wait. This isn't my ring.

HUSBAND 2: Not your ring? Of course it is, Doll.
Whose ring would it be?

WIFE: (Looks again at the ring, then looks over to
the sink. SHE quickly walks to the sink and picks
up the drainpipe, reaches her fingers in, and
pulls out another ring. SHE holds the ring up to her
face with her right hand, then lifts her left hand
up to her face to compare the rings.)
Not my ring.

HUSBAND 2: Why don't you quit monkeying
around and come back to the table. I need
some more bourbon.

(Coolio's song "GANGSTER'S PARADISE" begins
to play on the MP3 PLAYER.)

HUSBAND 2: Hold on now! Just what is that
noise?! Angel, find some music on the radio
before you sit down. You know the kind I like.

(The WIFE absently walks over to the MP3, presses
a button, and turns to face HUSBAND 2. "SING,
SING, SING" by Benny Goodman begins to play.)

HUSBAND 2: That's more like it! Now get back
over here and pour me another bourbon.

(The WIFE takes a long look at HUSBAND 2 and

then walks over to the sink. SHE stands in front of the sink and looks at the ring in her right hand. SHE turns and takes one more look at HUSBAND 2, then turns back to the sink, slides the ring off of her left hand, and throws both rings out of the window above the sink. SHE slowly turns around to face the table and sees that HUSBAND 2's chair is empty. SHE walks over to the MP3 player and presses a button. "NO MORE" by Billie Holiday begins to play. SHE sits back down in her chair, lifts her wine glass, smiles a broad smile, and toasts the empty chair across from her.)

DIM TO BLACK OUT

THE END

Stains & Blots #1
by Veronica Scharf Gracia
(Digital images, originally produced with
vegetable, flower and herb tinctures 5 x 7 in, 2019)

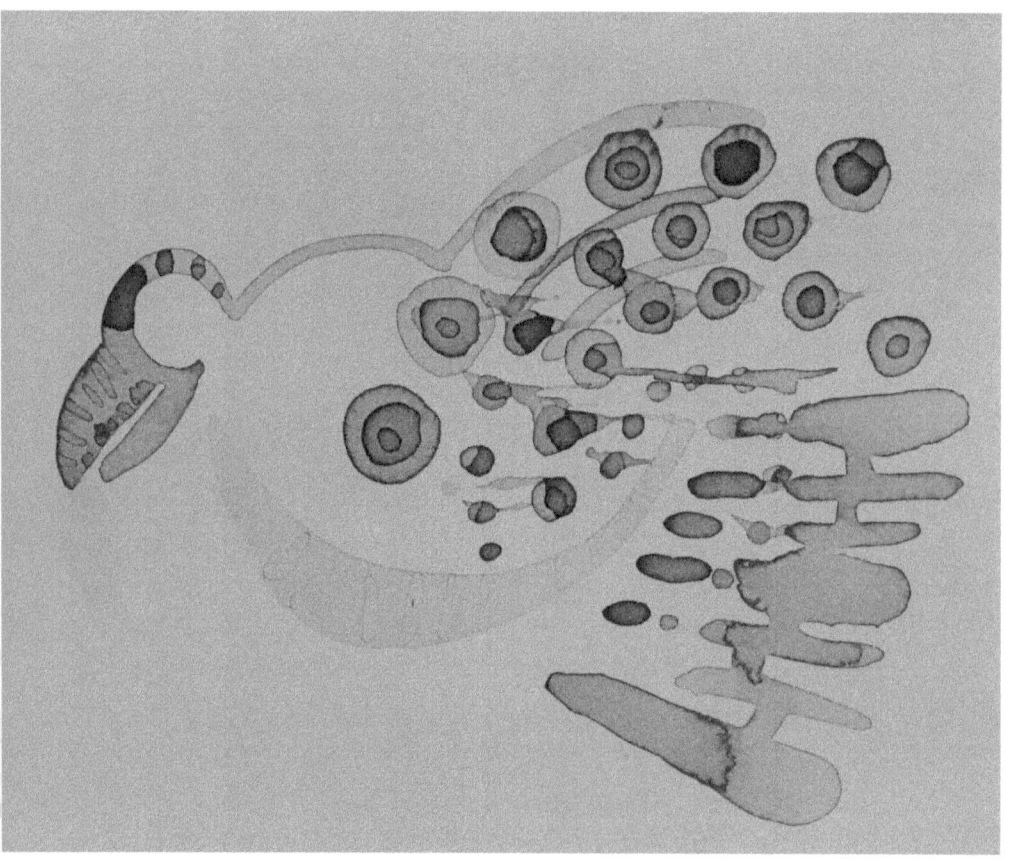

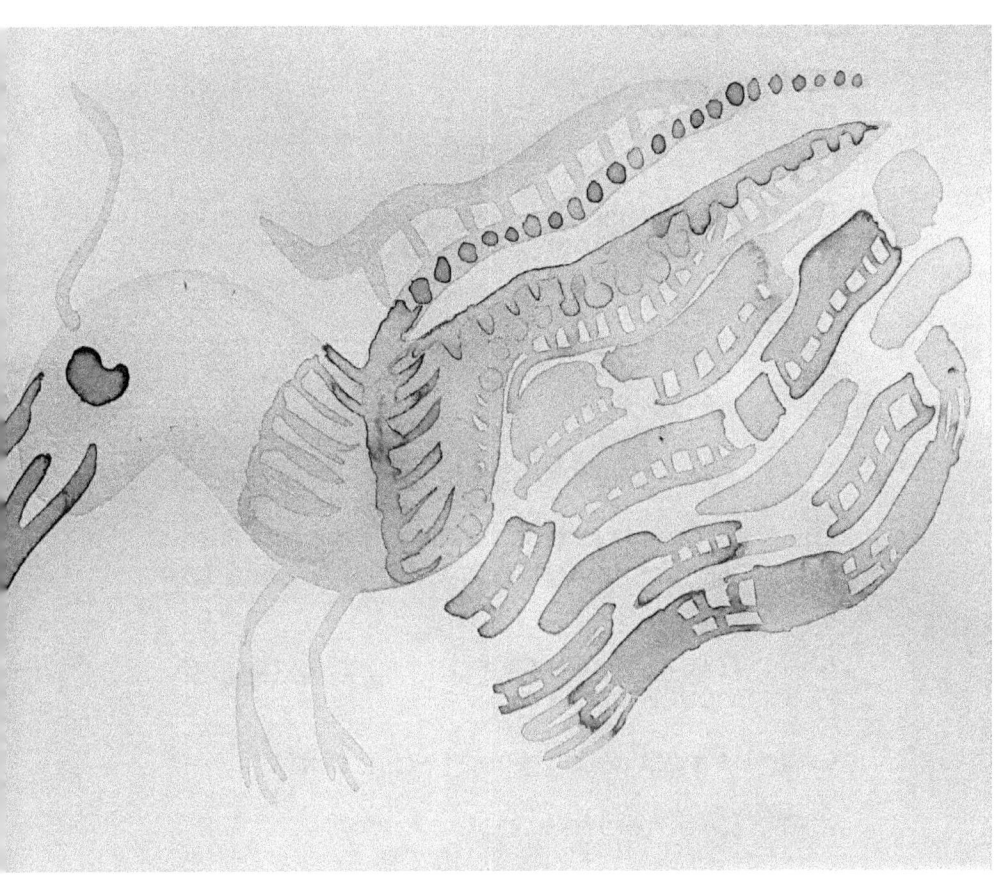

STAINS & BLOTS #4
BY VERONICA SCHARF GRACIA
(Digital images, originally produced with
vegetable, flower and herb tinctures 5 x 7 in, 2019)

SCENES

by PENNY JACKSON

SCENE 1

(A MAN in an office. A young GIRL in jeans and a t-shirt. On the MAN'S desk is a large and heavy golden award.)

MAN: So your mom had to sell her pickup truck.

GIRL: Our trailer.

MAN: Very unselfish of her.

GIRL: My sister had to change schools too. She really didn't want to move. She misses her school and her friends.

MAN: Your family sacrificed a lot for your career. What about your Dad?

GIRL: He's gone. Left when I was a baby.

MAN: So, no real man in your family?

GIRL: I guess so. But my mom is amazing. She can do anything.

MAN: Well she recognized your talent. That's for sure. So you think you can handle the pressure, working with such a big film star?

GIRL: I've always been his biggest fan! I have posters all over my wall.

MAN: This play has a huge budget and let's face it, you're unknown.

GIRL: That's why I'm so glad you chose me. I couldn't be more grateful.

MAN: The thing is, you never had a Dad.

GIRL: Right. So…

MAN: This is a play about fatherhood. Your father saves you. You need to feel gratitude and love for your father.

GIRL: Of course. I read the script.

MAN: Still, you haven't experienced those emotions for someone who is your Dad.

GIRL: I'm an actress.

MAN: Come here.

GIRL: Why?

MAN: I want to show you something.

(The GIRL walks hesitantly to him.)

MAN: Sit on my lap.

GIRL: Excuse me?

MAN: Prove to me that you know how to treat a father. My daughters always sit on my lap. Think of it as an acting exercise.

GIRL: I don't…

MAN: Prove it to me. I have other actresses just dying for this role. And we haven't finalized your contract.

(The GIRL stands in front of the MAN.)

GIRL: I need to call my mom.

MAN: And tell her you didn't get the role? That all

her sacrifices were for nothing? You'll never work in this town again.

(The GIRL walks to the MAN and sits on his lap.)

BLACKOUT.

(We only hear his murmurs of "Come on," and her protests.)

Suddenly, the lights RISE.

(The MAN is lying on the floor. It is unclear if he is alive or dead)

(The GIRL addresses the audience.)

GIRL: That was scene one. The usual producer scumbag trying to feel up a teenage actress and make her kneel to the floor and unzip his pants. But let's rewind this now...

SCENE 2

(The MAN stands and returns to his chair.)

MAN: The thing is, you never had a Dad.

GIRL: Right. So…

MAN: This is a play about fatherhood. Your father saves you. You need to feel gratitude and love for your father.

GIRL: Of course. I read the script.

MAN: Still, you haven't experienced those emotions for someone who is your Dad.

GIRL: I'm an actress.

MAN: Come here.

GIRL: Why?

MAN: I want to show you something.

(The GIRL walks hesitantly to him.)

MAN: Sit on my lap.

GIRL: Excuse me?

MAN: Prove to me that you know how to treat a father. My daughters always sit on my lap. Treat it as an acting exercise.

GIRL: I don't think...

MAN: Prove it to me. I have other actresses just dying for this role. And we haven't finalized your contract.

(The GIRL stands in front of the man).

GIRL: I need to call my mom. She said if you ever tried to do this shit to let her know.

MAN: Watch your mouth.

GIRL: You watch it. I know what happened to Leslie Salter. To Rachel Simmons. To Jackie Ash. You raped them.

MAN: Nothing was proven.

GIRL: Jackie Ash was thirteen years old.

MAN: Listen, you stupid bitch, you moronic cunt, I'll ruin you, I'll kill you.

(The MAN grabs the girl. They struggle but the GIRL manages to grab the award on his desk and smash it against his head. The MAN falls down to the floor, dead. The GIRL stares at him. Then she takes out her cell phone.)

GIRL: Jackie, are Rachel and Leslie there? Tell them I did it. He won't bother anyone ever again.

BLACKOUT.

(When the lights rise again, we see the man sitting at the desk. The GIRL turns to the audience.)

GIRL: This is Scene Three.

SCENE 3

MAN: Come here.

GIRL: Why?

MAN: I want to show you something.
(THE GIRL walks hesitantly to him.)

MAN: Sit on my lap.

GIRL: Excuse me?

MAN: Prove to me that you know how to treat a father. My daughters always sit on my lap. Treat it as an acting exercise.

GIRL: I don't think...

MAN: Prove it to me. I have other actresses just dying for this role. And we haven't finalized your contract.

(The GIRL stands in front of the man. She walks slowly in front of him about to sit on his lap. An older woman in a business suit enters. She is his assistant.)

OLDER WOMAN: What is she doing here?

MAN: Just having a chat about the film.

OLDER WOMAN: You know what Doug said about you being alone in your office with young actresses.
(to girl)You should leave.

GIRL: Yes.

(The GIRL exits.)

OLDER WOMAN: You know what your lawyer said. And the president of the board. Not to mention your lawyer.

MAN: I pay you to keep your mouth shut.

OLDER WOMAN: You pay me to keep you out of trouble.

MAN: She reminds me of you. When you first

came out and were auditioning for that role in the play that won the Tony.

OLDER WOMAN: And you know what happened.

MAN: So, I still can't ever see her?

OLDER WOMAN: I will never let my daughter see you.

MAN: Our daughter. If you hate me so much, why are you still here?

OLDER WOMAN: To protect girls like her.

BLACKOUT.

(Lights RISE. The GIRL addresses the audience while the MAN sits at his desk.)

GIRL: This is Scene Four. Or Five. Or Six. Choose any of them. People will say it never happened. Other people will swear it was even worse. Fake news. Consensual. Casting Couch. She knew. Of course she knew. What did she think would happen alone in a room with that man? But what if she was sixteen and her mother and sister gave up everything so she could be an actress? And she knew she was good. She knew she was better than good. And he knew he was bad. He was worse than bad.

SCENE 4

(The GIRL stands in front of the desk.)

MAN: Come here.

GIRL: Why?

MAN: I want to show you something.

(The GIRL walks hesitantly to him.)

MAN: Sit on my lap.

GIRL: Excuse me.

MAN: Prove to me that you know how to treat a father. My daughters always sit on my lap. Treat it as an acting exercise.

GIRL: I don't think...

MAN: Prove it to me. I have other actresses just dying for this role. And we haven't finalized your contract.

(The GIRL stands in front of the man.)

GIRL: I need to call my mom.

MAN: And tell her you didn't get the role? That all her sacrifices were for nothing? You'll never work in this town again.

GIRL: I'm gone.

(The GIRL exits. The MAN steps away from his desk and addresses the audience.)

MAN: Go ahead and blame me. Or blame the system. Or maybe blame yourselves. How many times did you know and not say anything? What did you see out of the corner of your eye? Hear behind closed doors? This is just a play. But outside this theater there are no actors. Outside this theater there is truth and there are lies. All these scenes are over. Go home and write one yourself. Be the author. But don't you dare applaud. We are not there yet.

THE END

SOCIAL NETWORK BY GEORGE L STEIN
(color photography 4272x2848, 2019)

BIOGRAPHIES
BIOGRAPHIES
BIOGRAPHIES
BIOGRAPHIES
BIOGRAPHIES
BIOGRAPHIES
BIOGRAPHIES
BIOGRAPHIES
BIOGRAPHIES
BIOGRAPHIES
BIOGRAPHIES
BIOGRAPHIES
BIOGRAPHIES
BIOGRAPHIES

PROSE

Carly Mastroni – Carly Mastroni is an MFA student at Lindenwood University. Her recent publications include essays in *Thin Air Magazine* and *Hippocampus Magazine*.

Micah L Thorp – Micah L Thorp is physician and writer in Portland, Oregon.

Rex Adams – Originally from Coulee City, Washington, Rex Adams now lives near Marsing, Idaho with his wife and two daughters. His work has appeared in *The Georgia Review, CRAFT, Sky Island Journal*, and elsewhere.

Robin Jeffrey – Robin Jeffrey was born in Cheyenne, Wyoming, to a psychologist and a librarian, giving her a love of literature and a consuming interest in the inner workings of people's minds, which have served her well as she pursues a career in creative writing. Robin has been published in *The Molotov Cocktail, Sky Island Journal, Cagibi, Silver Needle Press, The Esthetic Apostle, Prometheus Dreaming, Flumes Literary Journal, After Happy Hour Review*, and *The Mary Sue*. She currently resides in Bremerton, WA.

Shilo Niziolek – Shilo Niziolek is a graduate student in New England College's MFA program. Her nonfiction has appeared in the *Broad River Review, SLAB, Heartwood Literary Magazine, Persephone's Daughters, Litro Magazine, Oregon Humanities*, online publication *Beyond the Margins, VoiceCatcher, Buckman Journal, Burnt Pine Magazine, Fearsome Critters, DASH*, and the *Sandy River Review*.

Stephan Lang – Stephan Lang is a relatively new writer. His first three short stories were published in *BlazeVox, Gloom Cupboard*, and *Sixers Review*.

POETRY

Bina Ruchi Perino – Bina Ruchi Perino is a University of North Texas post-baccalaureate student, seeking a Bachelor of Arts in English, Creative Writing. Her work can be found in the *North Texas Review*, *The Nassau Review*, *Sink Hollow*, and more. She is forthcoming in *Digging through the Fat* and *Euphony Journal*.

Claudia Buckholts – Claudia Buckholts received Creative Writing Fellowships from the National Endowment for the Arts and Massachusetts Artists Foundation, and the Grolier Poetry Prize. Her work has appeared in *Alaska Quarterly Review*, *Indiana Review*, *Minnesota Review*, *New American Writing*, *Prairie Schooner*, *The Southern Review*, and other journals; and in two books, *Bitterwater* and *Traveling Through the Body*.

Debora Chappell – Debora Chappell lives in Denver, Colorado and frequently travels to New Mexico to visit family, friends, and fellow poets. She has a BA in English and an MA in Creative Writing-Poetry from The University of Denver. Her work has appeared in *The Denver Quarterly* and *2River View* (September 2019). She currently directs Vagabond Pony Writers Workshops.

Gwen Hart – Gwen Hart teaches writing at Buena Vista University in Storm Lake, Iowa. Her second poetry collection, *The Empress of Kisses*, won the X.J. Kennedy Poetry Prize from Texas Review Press.

Jack Donahue – Jack Donahue has published short stories and poems in *North Dakota Quarterly*; *Laldy* (Scotland), *Prole* (U.K.), *Poetry Salzburg Review* (Austria) *Armarolla* (Cypress), *Bindweed* (Ireland), *Opossum,* and others throughout North America, India and Europe. Mr. Donahue received his M.Div. degree from New Brunswick, Theological Seminary, NJ in 2008. He is married and resides on the North Fork of Long Island, NY.

Joanne Esser – Joanne Esser is the author of the poetry collection *Humming At The Dinner Table*, (November 2019), and the chapbook *I Have Always Wanted Lightning*, both from Finishing Line Press. She lives in Minneapolis, Minnesota and has been a teacher of young children for over thirty years. Recent work appears in *Passager, Miramar, Into the Void, Gyroscope Review* and *The Stillwater Review*, among other literary journals.

Louis P. Nappen – Louis P. Nappen, Esq., received his BA/MAT degrees from Monmouth University, where he served as editor-in-chief of the college newspaper and literary magazine. For several years, Nappen taught high school English/journalism, then attended Seton Hall University Law School. He is presently an attorney in a small firm focusing on constitutional and civil rights. Nappen's poetry has most recently been published by *The Offbeat Literary Journal* (Michigan State University), *Medusa's Laugh Press,* and *Temenos Journal* (Central Michigan University).

Ray Keifetz – Poems and stories by Ray Keifetz have recently appeared or are forthcoming in *The Bitter Oleander, Briar Cliff Review, Kestrel,* and Osiris. His debut collection, "Night Farming In Bosnia" was the winner of the Bitter Oleander Press Library of Poetry Award.

Sofia Martimianakis – Sofia completed her undergraduate degree in English Literature at the University of Toronto and her MA at the University of Waterloo. Her recent publications include fiction in *Cloudbank*, nonfiction in the *Rappahannock Review* and *Cleaning Up Glitter Magazine*, and poetry and photography in *Chaleur Magazine* and the *Tiny Seed Literary Journal*.

Stuart Forrest – Stuart James Forrest was born in Omaha, Nebraska in 1951. He is a retired public servant living in Oceanside, California. He can be contacted by email at, sturrtforrest@att.net. In the summer of 2014, he developed a passion for creative writing while attending Stanford University Continuing Studies. He continues writing poetry, short stories and hopes to develop enough skill to be a strong, creative voice of his generation of Black Americans who lived through a very tumultuous period in American history.

PLAYS

Kipp Knott – Kip Knott's writing has appeared in numerous journals and magazines, including *Barrow Street, Beloit Fiction Journal, Gettysburg Review, The Sun,* and *Virginia Quarterly Review.* He is the author of four poetry chapbooks, the most recent being *Afraid of Heaven* (Mudlark). His first full-length collection of poetry—*Tragedy, Ecstasy, Doom,* and *So On*—is forthcoming from Kelsay Books in 2020.

Penny Jackson – Penny Jackson's plays have been produced in New York City, Los Angeles, Chicago, Edinburgh, and Dublin. Her most recent production was *The Battles of Richmond Hills* produced at the Performing Arts Center in New York City. Her short play, *Before*, was chosen as one of the best short plays of 2016 by Applause Theater Books. Awards include a Pushcart Prize, a MacDowell Colony Fellowship and The Elizabeth Janeway in writing from Barnard College. She is a member of The Dramatist Guild and The League of Professional Theatre Women.

ARTWORK

Daniel A Ciochina – Daniel was born in Portland, Oregon as the first generation of his family to be born in the United States. He enjoys exploring South America, Europe, and the States while surveying the characteristics of society, people, objects, and their relations between each other. With this in mind he creates objects and pieces that embody these ideas. Making the viewers question or reflect their own stance within a given space or realm of thought.

Daniel Staub Weinberg – Daniel Staub Weinberg is a pen and ink wordartist focusing on politics and social issues. His work has been shown at Intuit Gallery, DANK Haus, Uptown Arts Center, Second Story Studios, and Uri-Eichen Galleryand others. Online he has been in *Toe Good, Meat for Tea, Alexandria Quarterly, Prometheus Dreaming, Cold Mountain Review, Blue Mesa Review and Blue Fifth Review* and others.

George L Stein – George L Stein is a writer and photographer living in Metropolis/NYC. George works in both film and digital formats in the urban decay, architecture, fetish, and street photography genres. His emphasis is on composition, with the juxtaposition of beauty and decay lying at the center of his aesthetic. George has been published in *Midwestern Gothic, Gravel, Foliate Oak, After Hours, Hoosier Lit, Gulf Stream Magazine, 3Elements, Stoneboat, Occulum, the Gnu Journal, Iliinot Review, and Darkside Magazine.*

Guilherme Bergamini – Reporter, photographer, and visual artist, Guilherme Bergamini is Brazilian and graduated in Journalism. For more than two decades, he has developed projects with photography and the various narrative possibilities that art offers. The works of the artist dialogue between memory and social political criticism. He believes in photography as having the aesthetic potential to become a transforming agent of society. Awarded in national and international competitions, Guilherme Bergamini participated in collective exhibitions in 22 countries.

Jodie Filan – Jodie Filan is an artist in Saskatoon, born and raised. She has been published in *RAR, Dark Ink press, Buddy Lit Zone, *82 Review, Aesthetica (Europe), Pithead Chapel, Nunum, Riza Press, Penultimate Peanut, The Raw Art Review (*Spring 2019), *High Shelf Press, Please See Me,* among others . Recently Ms. Filan also placed 6th in Fusion arts 4th annual B+W competition (May 2019) and a painting of hers was accepted at Art Lark in Albany, New York (Garibaldi Maritime Museum); and another at Greenway Art Festival. You can view her art page: www.facebook.com/jodiefilanart

Rebecca Ruth Gould – Rebecca Ruth Gould's chapbook is *Berlin-Damascus-Bethlehem* (Origami Poems Project, 2019). She translates from Persian, Russian, and Georgian, and has translated books such as *After Tomorrow the Days Disappear: Ghazals and Other Poems of Hasan Sijzi of Delhi* (Northwestern University Press, 2016) and *The Death of Bagrat Zakharych and other Stories* by Vazha-Pshavela (Paper & Ink, 2019). She was a finalist for the Luminaire Award for Best Poetry and (together with Kayvan Tahmasebian), Lunch Ticket's Gabo Prize (both in 2017), and is a Pushcart Prize nominee. Her photography has appeared in *Spill Words* and *Stonecrop.*

Veronica Scharf Garcia – Veronica Scharf Garcia born in Concepcion, Chile, grew up overseas in South America, Africa, the Middle East, and Europe. She continues her itinerant life now in Europe, her last home base was Los Angeles, California, two years ago. Scharf Garcia studied art at Colorado College and with Cristina Galvez in Lima, Peru. She has exhibited her art extensively and was selected as a Studio Artist at Bakehouse Art Complex, Deering Estate, Art Center/South Florida. Scharf Garcia has attended four residencies as Associate Artist, one sponsored by the Andy Warhol Foundation.

SUBMISSION INFORMATION
New Plains Review accepts original work in poetry, prose, and visual art. Submission information and editorial guidelines are accessible through the website.

ORDERING INFORMATION
Pricing for current and back issues are available through Amazon.

www.ingramcontent.com/pod-product-compliance
Lightning Source LLC
Chambersburg PA
CBHW071007120726
47910CB00004B/1418